ROYAL DARLING

KYLIE GILMORE

Royal Darling © 2019 by Kylie Gilmore

All rights reserved. No part of this publication may be reproduced, distributed, or transmitted in any form or by any means, including photocopying, recording, or other electronic or mechanical methods, without the prior written permission of the writer, except in the case of brief quotations embodied in critical reviews and certain other noncommercial uses permitted by copyright law.

This book is a work of fiction. Names, characters, places, brands, media, and incidents are the product of the author's imagination or are used fictitiously. The author acknowledges the trademarked status and trademark owners of various products referenced in this work of fiction, which have been used without permission. The publication/use of these trademarks are not authorized, associated with, or sponsored by the trademark owners. Any resemblance to actual events, locales, or persons, living or dead, is purely coincidental.

First Edition: May 2019

Cover design by Michele Catalano Creative

Published by: Extra Fancy Books

ISBN-10: 1-942238-88-6

ISBN-13: 978-1-942238-88-1

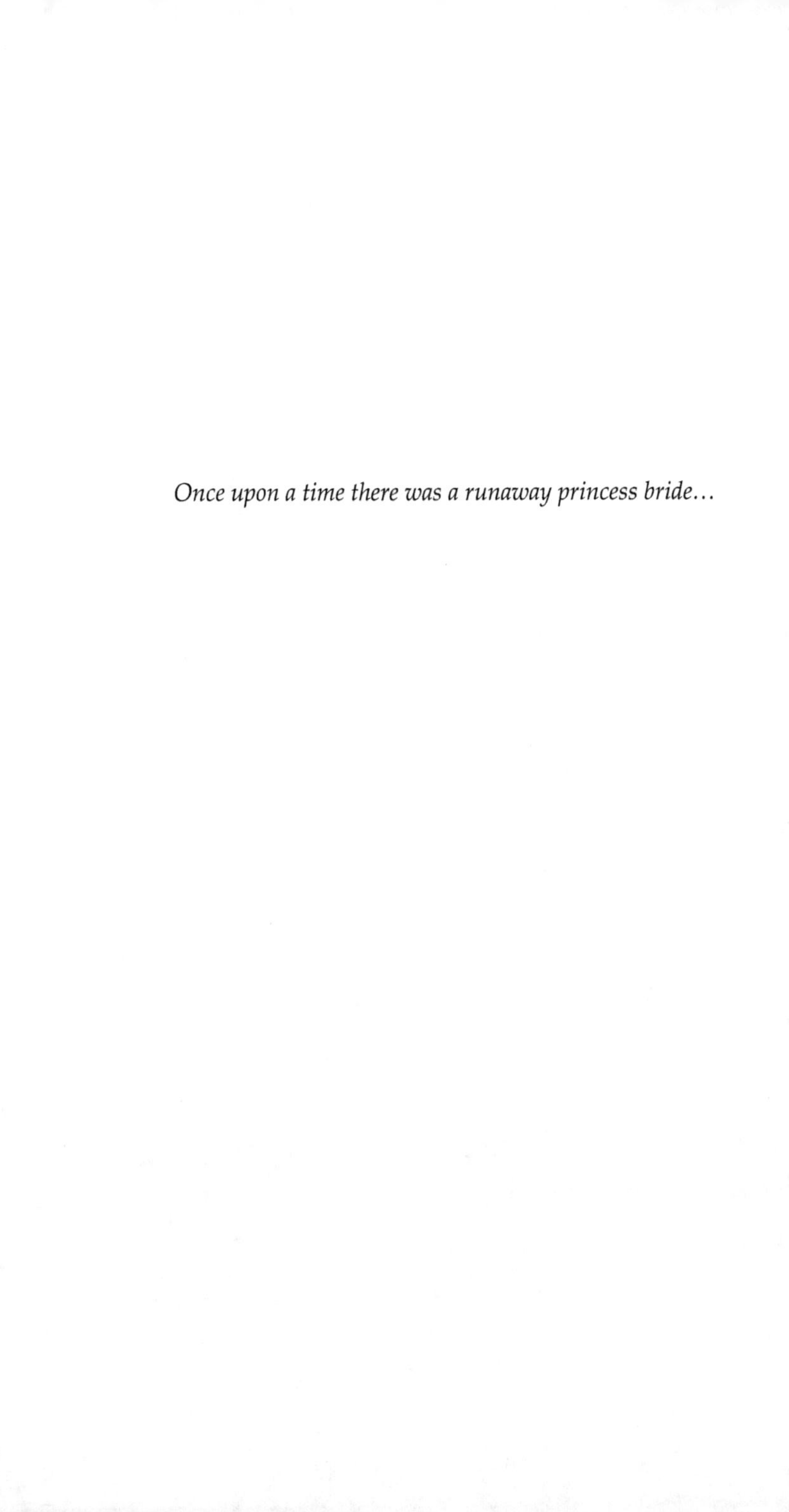

Once upon a time there was a runaway princess bride…

1

Emma

Tomorrow I will marry a man I've met only twice.

The first time I was sixteen, shortly after our engagement, and the second time was this week to prepare for our wedding. This is normal for an arranged marriage between two far-flung kingdoms. I smooth a shaky hand through my hair. My nerves are misplaced. I'm Princess Emma Rourke of Villroy Island, fifth in line to the throne and firstborn daughter. I was raised to be proper, stoic, and to adhere strictly to royal protocol. I must rise to the occasion.

I am really quite fortunate in my parents' choice of husband for me. Crown Prince Abdul Marjan of Kainei is only a year older than me at twenty-six, and he's handsome with dark brown hair neatly parted to the side, chocolate brown eyes, and a bright white toothy smile. He was educated in England and has been a perfect gentleman during his visit this week. After our marriage, I will move to Kainei, a prosperous kingdom in Southeast Asia.

There is simply no reason for concern.

The wedding rehearsal in the palace chapel begins soon, but before I dress for the occasion, I decide to check in on my mother in her private suite. I think she would be pleased with my regal poise during this week of social functions. She hasn't attended any of them, wanting to be alone in her grief. My father died three months ago. I miss my father, we all do. He was the king, and a large vibrant presence in my life before the cancer that ultimately took him. My mother abdicated the throne upon his death, not wanting to lead without him.

I take a deep breath, working for the perfect composure expected of me, before knocking on her door.

My mother's maid, Joan, answers, bowing her head and dropping into a deep curtsy. "Your Highness."

"Is my mother awake?"

Joan steps back. "Yes, ma'am, though she's still in bed."

I let out a breath. I had hoped my wedding would bring her out of her reclusive state. I wish there was something I could do to help her. I pass through the formal sitting room to her bedroom, where she's propped up on pillows in a large antique mahogany bed in near darkness, the only light the glow of the TV mounted on the wall. The volume is so low, I'm not sure she can hear it. I turn on the small lamp on her nightstand and glance at the screen. It's the reality show she used to watch with my father.

She slowly turns to look at me and murmurs, "Hello," before turning back to the TV.

My heart sinks. She's in her pale blue silk robe, her dark brown hair out of its usual neat chignon, loose over her shoulders as though she no longer cares about her appearance. She used to always be dressed in perfectly tailored pastel dresses, fully made up and accessorized. Her hazel eyes have bags under them; her skin is too pale. She hasn't been outdoors, except for the funeral, in more than a year. She remained at my father's side while he was bedridden. I have her same coloring, though my skin isn't so pale. I enjoy my time outdoors on Villroy.

I bend to kiss her cheek. "Mother, my wedding rehearsal is tonight. Will you join us for dinner after?"

"I will be at the wedding," she says, her voice rough, like she hasn't spoken for a while.

I sit next to her on the bed and take her cool hand. "I'm leaving soon. I fear I'm ill prepared. I'm not yet fluent in Malay. Everything will be so different there."

She doesn't respond.

"I'm scared," I admit softly.

She finally looks at me and gives my hand a firm squeeze. "You're not scared. You're nervous, which is to be expected. You must rise above."

"Yes, Mother." I know this. Why is it so difficult? I've spent my life rising to the high expectations of my mother and been rewarded with a close bond. I was the daughter she longed for after four sons. I was the daughter she was proud of. Now she feels so far away. "I wish you could've attended more of this week's functions. Are you sure you won't join us for dessert, maybe?"

She releases my hand and turns back to the TV. "I'm not ready to appear in public. I will be there tomorrow for the ceremony."

My chest constricts, making it hard to breathe. I understand she's grieving, but I can't help but feel the loss of her in my life. I'd imagined this to be a joyous time, where she was happily joining me for all the pre-wedding preparations, the ultimate mother-daughter bonding time. Some small part of me had hoped she'd prepare me for what lies ahead, since she's been through the same, traveling halfway around the world from a small island kingdom off the coast of Australia to Villroy Island, just off the coast of southwestern France, to marry my father, a man she'd never met before their wedding day.

When my parents broached the topic of an arranged marriage when I was sixteen, explaining that it was the traditional way, and asking if I'd agree to their choice of groom, I readily complied. It wasn't mandatory; most of my older siblings had opted against it, except for the heir, Gabriel, who was held to a higher standard. The truth is, I *wanted to* carry on tradition, and I was proud to know I would be helping Villroy with a useful alliance. Knowing my parents also had an arranged marriage that turned to love, I was content in my decision. But now that it's here, shortly after my twenty-fifth birthday, as my parents required, I'm fighting to keep my composure. And, it pains me to admit it, but I am having doubts. I will be living with a stranger in a foreign land, one I have never visited. I will miss my family, my palace home, my island. Villroy Island is a part of me with its blue-green sea, rocky cliffs, and soft sand beaches. I've spent many a happy time on Villroy. My future happiness is uncertain.

My mother speaks so softly I have to lean close to catch the words. "You must turn to your husband now for your comfort."

Tears sting my eyes. I understand she's trying to help by pushing me toward my future husband, but it hurts. I bury all my worries, my fears, my doubts down deep. I will not be sharing them with Abdul. I must be brave. I stand and do a quick curtsy. "I will see you tomorrow."

She inclines her head, but her gaze remains riveted on the TV.

I turn and rush from the room, heading upstairs to my own suite to dress. My lower lip trembles, and I bite it, willing myself to rise above. This will all be over soon. I will adjust to my new life. I am my mother's daughter—strong, stoic, proud—and I will do what's right for my kingdom. My marriage will forge an alliance that will greatly benefit Villroy's faltering economy and ensure a stable future. I will honor my mother and make her proud by following through with my parents' wishes.

My maid, Lina, is waiting, my clothes already laid out. She's efficient and competent, so it takes little time until I'm ready for the wedding rehearsal. Or maybe I just feel like it's quick because I secretly wish for a delay.

"You look beautiful, Your Highness," she says. "That color suits you."

"Thank you," I say absently. My modest long-sleeved pale

rose dress with a delicate overlay of lace is beautiful. My wardrobe has always been modest and proper, favoring pastels, my shoulders and cleavage always covered, the hemlines ending at the knees. My wedding gown is a gorgeous but modest confection of silk, lace, and tulle. Even my wedding night lingerie is modest, a white full-length slip with a matching robe. My mind flashes to what, if anything, I might feel on my wedding night for my new husband. He hasn't touched me, not even to hold my hand. He doesn't know I'm not a virgin, that I once experienced passion. I will tell him the truth if he seems understanding of young reckless actions, but if his expectation is a virgin bride—a possibility in a traditional kingdom such as his—I have a lie at the ready. I always think quick on my feet.

I cross to the bedroom window and gaze at the sea, the familiar view soothing me. They cannot begin rehearsal without the bride, so if I take a few extra moments to compose myself, it will be fine.

"Will there be anything else, Your Highness?" Lina asks.

It's on the tip of my tongue. *Am I making a mistake?* I turn from the view. "Nothing else, Lina. Thank you."

She bows her head, does a quick curtsy, and leaves, the door quietly closing behind her.

I tell myself to move, one foot in front of the other. My body doesn't cooperate, so I take a deep breath, closing my eyes. Someone knocks. Lina must've decided to ask if I'd like an escort to the palace chapel. I once imagined it would be my mother by my side.

"Come in, Lina."

The door opens slowly, and my sister-in-law, Anna, with her wild mass of dark curls, pokes her head in. "Got a minute?"

I gesture her in, then do a quick head bow and a deep curtsy.

"Please, Emma, you don't need to curtsy to me in the privacy of your room."

I bite back a smile, mildly amused at the way she keeps

forgetting she outranks me. She's now the queen of Villroy, ever since she married Gabriel two months ago.

"You are my queen," I remind her. She's an American, who's had to learn the royal protocol.

She steps close and lowers her voice. "Do you want to talk?"

"About what?"

She smiles gently, her brown eyes warm. "Emma, getting married is a big deal, especially when it's an arranged marriage you agreed to sight unseen when you were only sixteen." Since the age of sixteen, I have faltered only once from my chosen path, and the crushing heartbreak of that misstep made me come to my senses. Passion only goes so far.

I paste on a polite smile. "My parents had an arranged marriage that turned out beautifully. I'm sure it will be just the same for me. Abdul is everything I could want in a husband."

"Do you love him?"

I steel my nerves. "I will learn to love him."

She jabs a finger at me. "That is your mother talking."

"That is me talking," I snap. She doesn't understand my mother or our bond. The two of them are like oil and water.

She sighs. "There's a silver Renault Clio parked on the service road by the side of the chapel, the keys under the mat, in case you'd like to get away and think."

I blink, surprised at her insight, knowing I might need a break from the pre-wedding preparations. Still, I can't admit to my nerves. She's so brash and outspoken, she'd want to…I don't know what, but she's capable of anything. The woman single-handedly came up with a brilliant plan to transform our dying fishing industry into a manufacturer of natural beauty products featuring fish oil, algae, sponges, sea salt and the like to be used and sold at a new day spa on Villroy. The success of the venture is uncertain since it's still in the planning stages, but there's no denying its potential. And the fundraiser to kick off those plans—all her idea—was a royal bachelor auction featuring my single brothers! Quite scandalous! I heard my brothers showed some skin, flashing pecs and abs. Lucas even caused a riot by preparing to unbuckle his belt. My brothers have been given freedoms I was not, and are not nearly so proper as me. Gabriel, the heir, being the exception. Is it no wonder I look up to him?

But with the rehearsal tonight, followed by dinner, and the wedding tomorrow, I don't have time to get away and think. Besides, thinking will only lead to more nerves. I need to be stronger than that.

I lift my chin. "No need, but thank you. Now I must get to the rehearsal."

"I'll go with you."

I stifle a sigh, knowing Anna won't let the topic go. She's used to speaking her mind, and Gabriel indulges her. She's changed him. Gabriel isn't as proper anymore. He's relaxed about a lot of royal protocol; even his demeanor has changed. He smiles a lot, his posture less rigid. Between the change in Gabriel and my mother withdrawing from royal life and duties, I've been adrift. They were my role models. A small voice in my head whispers that my rigid adherence to royal protocol and tradition is no longer needed or appreciated. But who am I without the rules I've lived my life by?

I square my shoulders and straighten my spine, maintaining a composed pleasant expression as I walk down the hallway with Anna.

"Gabriel married me for love," she says. "He turned down his arranged marriage." She knows I'm partial to Gabriel.

I say nothing. This is not news.

She grabs me by the arm, startling me. No one ever grabs a princess. Her grip is tight, her voice urgent. "I wish you the kind of happiness I share with Gabriel. Please, Emma, if you have any doubts at all, even just a tiny little hint of a doubt, then we'll postpone." She whispers directly in my ear, "Or cancel. I'll smooth it over, make amends where needed."

I swallow hard, my heart thundering in my chest. Do I

dare break from the royal tradition I eagerly agreed to? To call a halt after all this planning? After Abdul has waited nine long years for me?

She whispers fiercely, "This is your life not your mother's." I don't like her talking about my mother like she controls me. I love my mother.

I yank my arm from her grasp. "Do not speak of this again."

She sighs but remains quiet. We reach the stairs, where Gabriel and Abdul are waiting at the bottom. Gabriel's eyes light up in anticipation of her arrival. Abdul gives me a small close-lipped smile, and I reciprocate.

We begin the descent to our respective men. She whispers under her breath, "The car will remain waiting for you any time you need it."

"I won't need it," I whisper back.

She smiles at Gabriel and speaks under her breath. "You're as stubborn as Gabriel."

I smile too. "Thank you."

Then I take my place with my groom.

"You look beautiful," he says, as he's said every time he sees me.

"Thank you," I say modestly, eyes downcast.

"Shall we go?"

"Yes, of course."

He doesn't offer his arm or take my hand, merely walks by my side as we make the long trek toward the chapel at the end of the west wing. Behind us, Gabriel, Anna, and Abdul's entourage of family members and servants follow at a sedate pace.

"I'm looking forward to showing you around Kainei," Abdul says. "I'm sure you'll feel quite at home, though it is a great deal hotter than here."

"I also look forward to it," I reply.

We continue on in silence, my mind skipping ahead, trying to imagine my new life. The picture won't come into view, my mind a blank. I focus on Abdul instead. Will he be pleased or disappointed in his new bride? Will he take a mistress after I produce the expected heir for his kingdom? I would like a child. The rest is uncertain. For so long I imagined my time as a bride as a magical romantic experience, imagined my future groom as quite taken with me. It's time to drop the fantasy.

I take one step into the gorgeous chapel with its soaring ceiling and abundance of gold trim and hand-painted stucco and go cold all over. The once welcoming space with its familiar marble statues, three silver pipe organs, hand-carved pews, and the long beautiful aisle with the red runner suddenly feels stifling. My breathing accelerates as the walls close in on me. Anna has gotten in my head, making my already frayed nerves even worse.

I refuse to look at her, refuse to look at my groom. I focus entirely on the minister at the end of the aisle and make my way forward woodenly, one foot in front of the other.

I make it through the rehearsal in a dignified, composed fashion.

I keep up my part of polite conversation through the rehearsal dinner, excusing myself early to prepare for bed. The strain of the day catches up to me, and I'm asleep within minutes.

The next day I wake refreshed and ready to begin the rest of my life. It was simply cold feet. Of course I can do this. It will be lovely.

I dress with the help of several maids and my younger sister, Silvia. My mother doesn't make an appearance, saying she can only handle going to the ceremony. I push down the hurt. She will see me doing my duty, as she did, and this will make her proud.

I step in front of the full-length mirror and take in me as a bride. It's suddenly so real. My hair is swept into an updo, the veil perched on top, my expression pinched. I attempt to relax my expression, but it's not possible. My breathing is shallow, my hands clammy, as I take in the dress I was once so excited about. It's very traditional, white silk with an overlay of lace up to my neck and down the long sleeves. It cinches at the waist, which is the top of a full fluffy bell shape made up of layers of tulle. The gown pools over my feet because it's meant to be worn with heels and I'm still in my slippers. I pull the veil over my face to get the full effect, and the world dims, the happy chatter of the women behind me drowned out by the buzzing in my ears. I go numb. I'm floating above it all, watching from a great distance, the princess bride about to be married.

"You look beautiful, ma'am," Lina says, appearing by my side. "The *perfect* bride! Would you like your shoes now?"

Perfect princess. Perfect bride.

I jolt back to reality, my gut churning, a restless surge of energy rushing down my legs. I whirl. "Excuse me, I need a moment to myself."

The maids rush from the room, and my sister, Silvia, blows me a kiss before heading out. I pull the veil back from my face and decide a walk is in order. I'm not expected in the chapel for an hour.

I lift my gown and head down the long hallway before taking a circuitous route to the ballroom, working to avoid where Abdul and his family are staying. If I could just see the reception area, imagine myself there as a happy bride celebrating my marriage, then all will be well.

Thankfully, the ballroom is empty. It's lovely as always with its glossy inlaid wooden floors, crystal chandeliers, frescoed ceiling paintings, and gold-leaf wallpaper. I can imagine the musicians over there and the dancing in the center, likely a waltz, elegant and regal. Long tables line one side of the room, set up with chafing dishes, and on the other side is a long table with a gargantuan tiered wedding cake in the center. I move as if in a dream, drawn to that wedding cake with the porcelain couple on top under an arch of tiny white flowers.

It is my likeness and Abdul's. We're smiling, looking for all the world in love. A high-pitched ringing sounds in my ears, my entire body overheating as I stare at the porcelain couple. Why did they make us look like this? We should appear proud, dignified, regal. Not in love. It's a distortion of reality. A *lie*. The decoration blurs in front of my eyes. Suddenly it looks like Abdul's laughing at me. A mockery. An *insult*.

I lunge forward to grab the mocking Abdul, and the decoration goes flying, bouncing off the back of the table and onto the wooden floor. *Oh no!* I hurry around to the other side of the table and stare at the damage. My head broke off and there are several chips missing from my gown.

It's a sign.

Marrying Abdul will be the end of me.

My head lifts. There's a car waiting by the side of the chapel.

Adrenaline rushes through me, my mind racing right along with my pulse. I grab the end of my gown and run straight out the door, booking it through the courtyard and around the back of the chapel to FREEDOM!

2

———

I tear off my veil and toss it behind some shrubbery. I'm a fugitive now. The old Renault is waiting as promised. I grab the keys from under the mat, scramble in, start it, and take off. I'm outside myself again, watching the scene unfold, only this time my mind is sharp. I have limited time before anyone notices I'm missing, and I'm extremely recognizable as a runaway bride in my gown. They'll be expecting me to go far away from the palace, so I will outmaneuver them and return to it through the servants' entrance!

I make the short drive around the front of the palace and park in the small lot next to identical Renaults the servants use for errands, along with bicycles. I slip into the side door belowstairs and race through the servants' hallway toward another set of stairs. Most of the servants will be busy assisting the guests and working in the kitchen. I look for young Christina's room, a new maid that Lina told me had worn a wig to emulate Anna, the queen. The servants gave her such a ribbing she hadn't worn it again. I poke my head in several rooms until I see it—a brown curly-haired wig on top of the dresser. I rush in, lock the door, and grab the servant's uniform of white shirt and black trousers from her closet. I change and steal some socks, along with her sensible black shoes, which are a little tight but do the job. Then I grab the wig and pull it on over my sleek updo. I roll the gown into a tight ball, tuck it under my arm, and take off for my own room.

I am a secret palace spy on a covert mission, gliding along undetected, stealthily avoiding wandering servants, outsmarting them all.

As soon as I get to my room, I lock the door. My heart is pounding so hard I swear it's going to burst through my chest. I drop the gown down the laundry chute. By the time it's discovered downstairs in the pile of sheets and towels, I'll be long gone. I shake my head at myself. They'll notice I'm missing long before they worry about the gown. And the broken porcelain couple might be a clue too. Ha! So smart I'm making no sense. Sheer panic clouds my thinking, but one thing is clear, I must escape!

I rush to my closet and freeze, unsure what I want. A purse! I grab the closest one and race around the room to all my hiding spots, stuffing cash, jewelry, passport, and phone into it.

Several exhilarating minutes later, I steal a bike from the service lot and pedal down the winding palace road. Not too fast, not too slow. I'm a servant now on a palace errand. There's noise in the distance, people shouting. The press? My family? Abdul's family? I can't linger to find out. I pedal faster. It's a downhill road, and I pick up speed quickly. I grip the handlebars tight, my mind already a step ahead. I'll go to the port, find an unoccupied boat, and hide. I just need some space to think. They'll be expecting me to take the yacht off the island, so I shouldn't be disturbed on a random boat.

As soon as I arrive at the port, I stash the bicycle behind an old warehouse used by the fishermen, and peek out at the dock, scanning the available boats. I give myself a few moments to catch my breath and clear my mind. The second I calm, guilt stabs at me. My God, what have I done? Poor Abdul will be so humiliated. His entire family is here. The press. I just did something *so bad*. I *have* to hide. I can't face him or anyone.

I swallow hard. The larger fishing vessels are out to sea. What's left are the smaller white boats of the locals, bobbing in the water, and a houseboat with a large enclosed cabin and a purple flag of a seahorse. That flag tells me it's probably a family's houseboat, definitely friendly, and most importantly, perfect for hiding.

I dart out from behind the warehouse and head straight for the friendly houseboat. It's anchored with a gangway, so it's no trouble at all to board. I peek in through the windows of the cabin. It appears to be empty. Yes! It's fate.

I try the cabin door. Locked. Luckily, I know what to do thanks to my ex. I pull a pin from my hair and pick the lock, letting myself in. The inside is messy. There's a brown U-shaped sofa surrounding a square wooden table littered with a plate, cup, fork, crumpled napkin, and a laptop. The adjacent small galley kitchen has a large box of Cocoa Puffs cereal left out on the counter. Definitely a family here.

I do a quick tour of the rest of the cabin to be sure there's no surprise visitors lurking. There's another small seating area around front, which is empty. Past the kitchen is a bedroom with a double bed, dressers on either side of it. The bed is unmade, and there's man clothes scattered about the floor. I'm sure the wife's clothes are in the hamper, where they belong. There's a tiny bathroom with just enough room for a toilet, a sink, and a shower nozzle hooked to the wall. A wonderfully empty refuge.

I heave a sigh of relief, wander back to the living room, and just stand there. What the hell did I just do? Running away? I might have to leave my old life behind forever. I've disgraced my family and dishonored my arrangement with Abdul. I clutch my shaking hands together.

A mostly full bottle of tequila and a shot glass on the kitchen counter catch my eye. I need to steady my nerves.

I help myself to a shot of tequila. *Gah!* It burns, it burns. *Whoa. Hey, now.* I'm suddenly relaxed. I don't think I've been this relaxed in a week. Maybe ever. Probably didn't help that I haven't eaten today because of my frazzled nerves. Instead I downed three cups of chamomile tea in hopes of calming myself. An impossible feat and much too much to ask of tea.

It hits me with a shock—I am free. The heavy burden of my obligation is lifted. I hadn't realized until this very moment how bad I felt before.

I lift my arms in a bold declaration. "Let's get pissed, snockered, two sheets to the wind!" I'm not sure if I'm using the slang right, but it sounds wonderfully coarse. Like something the guards or servants would say when they thought none of us royals were within earshot.

A proper princess never indulges in hard liquor and absolutely never drinks to excess. I am no longer a proper princess. I'm shocked at how good it feels to be free.

I down another shot, enjoying the burn this time. I am definitely loving this relaxed feeling. I do a little relaxed walk. No more wooden legs. I smile for no reason at all. Boy, I'm hungry. I grab the box of Cocoa Puffs, open it up, and pour it directly in my mouth. I haven't had these since university. So delicious! I pour some more into my mouth and chew heartily. I miss a few and little chocolate balls roll down my shirt, inside my shirt, and onto the floor. I extricate a few from my strapless bra (meant to go with my wedding gown) and chow down. What a wonderful invention—Cocoa Puffs. They should serve this at the palace. Suddenly my eyes sting, and I scrunch them tight, my mood diving to despair. I might never have breakfast at the palace again.

I do another shot and grip the counter, the room swaying. I need to figure out what's next.

I can't hide on this boat forever. I can't travel easily either. The press will be all over me. The only escape is with a brand-new identity. I can't use my passport. I need a fake ID like Anna's friend Polly had when she was a princess-in-hiding. That's me now. Though Polly is on probation, narrowly escaping jail time for identity theft.

I don't want to go to jail!

My day catches up to me, all the tension of the previous week, the rush of adrenaline from my escape, the loss of what I left behind. It's all too much. I stumble to the bedroom with its messy bed and curl up under the blankets. I lost Father; I feel like I lost Mother; I'm at sea, literally and figuratively. Everything is different at home with the change in leadership. I don't know where I belong anymore. Not with Abdul, I know that much. Who am I outside the palace? I can't just be a proper princess. There must be more to me.

My throat clogs with emotion, and the dam bursts. I cry for the loss of my father, for the loss of my mother's love, for the loss of me and my old life. So. Much. Loss. Mercifully, the tequila kicks in, and I'm out like a light.

I slowly wake to a warm press of something against my lips. A kiss. I'm Sleeping Beauty awakened with a kiss by my handsome prince. How lovely. Wait! It's not Abdul here to drag me back to the altar, is it? My eyes fly open in alarm, and I jerk upright, pulling the covers up to my chin, my head spinning with the sudden movement.

There's a blond man sitting on the bed next to my hip. Not Abdul. His features swim in front of my eyes, and I blink him into focus. He doesn't look like someone's father. He's maybe thirty with shaggy blond hair, blue eyes, a straight nose, and a beard in need of a trim. His long-sleeved gray thermal shirt pulls tight across wide shoulders and curving biceps. There's a bit of an edge to him, a tightly coiled power that seems a little dangerous. Though he did kiss me. I think. Something touched my lips. Maybe he was checking if I was breathing with his fingertips.

"I'm alive," I say, forcing my voice to sound confident and sure. "Hello."

"Hello, luv, get off my boat." His accent is British. His voice is deep, gravelly, and somehow strangely familiar.

My mind does a crazy whirl through the fuzziness of sleep and tequila, trying to remember the details between running from my own wedding to how I got here in this stranger's bed.

He reaches out one big hand and yanks the blankets out of my grip. A flash of a tattooed eagle on the inside of his wrist catches my eye. I glance down at myself. I'm in the servant's uniform. The details come flooding back. I made an escape worthy of a first-class spy, donning a maid's uniform, pedaling to the port, and hiding out on a family's houseboat. No, apparently, it's *his* houseboat.

He stands and hitches his thumb toward the door. He's not much for manners, though, to be fair, I am a stowaway. He's tall, more than six feet, sinewy with muscle, his long legs in black jeans with scuffed black boots.

I scramble for a suitable reason for being here as I swing my legs over the edge of the mattress. I manage to stand upright with minimal room spin, but then my gut churns horrifically, bile rising in my throat. "Excuse me."

I race to the tiny bathroom just outside the room and make it in time to toss my Cocoa Puffs. *Gross.* My misdeeds are in full evidence. Not my finest hour. Tequila was a terrible idea. I heave again and again.

"Are you okay?" he asks from the doorway.

Gah! No witnesses! I crawl over, slam the door, lock it, and hurry back to puke up the rest of my stomach.

Once I finish, I feel well enough to freshen up, helping myself to the sparse items I find in a small cabinet. I get a shock, seeing myself in the mirror in a brown curly wig. I'd forgotten about it. It's slightly askew, so I fix it. Then I brush my teeth with my finger and swish with mouthwash.

I open the door and find him sitting in the living room. The table is now cleared of dishes, and he's watching something on his laptop. His gaze snaps to mine, and it hits me why he sounded familiar. It's Jackson Walker. He's the guitarist and lead singer of Ignite. They played at the Cancer Research Foundation charity event I emceed in London. His raucous music jangled my nerves. His performance was wild, sweaty, and animal, which both appalled and fascinated me. He was unlike any man I'd ever seen before and never thought I'd see again. A rock god. A legendary bad boy.

My complete opposite.

He crooks his finger at me, and I approach, careful not to move my throbbing head too much.

I attempt a smile, hoping he's not about to kick me off the boat. I just need some time to think. I made an epic mess of everything and I'm not ready to face Abdul, my family, and his family until I have a clear plan on how to handle things. "Yes?"

He doesn't smile back. "You chundered in the loo and mucked up the kitchen. Well done. Piss off now." He jerks his head toward the door.

I slowly turn to peek at the kitchen and turn back to him. "The kitchen is clean."

"I swept up the Cocoa Puffs. Did you get any in the bowl?" He sounds extremely aggrieved.

I keep my straight-from-the-box-cereal-eating method to myself. "You'll be happy to know I left the bathroom just as I found it. Less a little of your toothpaste and mouthwash." I take a seat across from him, pleased that my brain is functioning again.

He looks less than pleased as he leans forward, resting his arms on the table in front of me. His sleeves are pushed up, revealing muscular tanned forearms. His voice is sharp, his gaze direct. "I don't do groupies anymore."

I can't help my smile. He thinks I'm a groupie. I must really be blending in already, no more proper princess image. I force myself to stop smiling, smashing my lips together. I don't want to look like an idiot.

He stares at my mouth and then jerks his gaze up to my eyes. "I'm going on a long trip, solo, yeah? So again, get off my boat. How did you even get in here? I locked it."

I bite my bottom lip, a plan formulating in my mind. "For how long?"

His brows shoot up. "How long do I want you gone? Forever."

Rude. I suppose I can put up with a lack of manners since he's ideal in other ways. "I meant how long is your trip?"

His eyes go half-mast. "For as long as I feel like."

"Where are you going?"

He exhales sharply. "If I tell you, will you leave?"

I nod and instantly regret it, wincing.

He drums his fingers on the table before finally saying, "France."

"Oh! I speak French."

"Actually, it's Italy."

"I speak Italian too."

He narrows his blue eyes. "China."

"I speak Mandarin."

He stands, goes to the cabin door, and opens it. "Good for you. Goodbye."

I stand, take one step toward the door, and stop. This is it. My one and only chance at a reprieve. I'm not ready for marriage. I've barely lived. I need a taste of a different life. The kind that comes naturally to him.

He's the antidote to my life of propriety.

The key to unlocking the new improper Emma. What luck to stumble upon his houseboat!

I seize the moment in a display of wild optimism and desperation. "I just quit my job at the palace. Are you in need of a servant?"

$$3$$

Jackson

A servant? Is she kidding me with this shite? First off, I don't have servants, well, unless you count my manager, but half the time it feels like I'm working for him, not the other way round. Second, does she think I'm a bloody idiot? Everyone knows her. I've seen her on tons of glossy magazines, gossip rags, and all over the internet. She's well known for her charitable works and her engagement to a wealthy future sultan. Princess Emma Rourke with her posh Villroy accent, all proper English with a hint of French cadence. She introduced our band at the Cancer Research Foundation event in London. I swallow down the lump in my throat, remembering that night. We'd just lost our keyboardist, Charlie, to a drug overdose. I was out of my mind in an agony of grief that I poured into the music. He was like a brother to me.

I glare at her perfect face with its big innocent hazel eyes, perky nose, and pink-tinged cheeks for that unwelcome reminder. Her long straight dark brown hair is currently hidden under a very unflattering curly wig. I bet she's a virgin with those innocent eyes, her prim and proper attitude, and the fact that she's been engaged since she was sixteen. Her fiancé looks just as proper; they probably never moved past holding hands. I have zero interest in a virgin princess. I haven't been with a virgin since I was a teenager and I was an arse about it, only caring that I got off. And I know I don't deserve someone as highborn as her. I come from nothing, and I never stick with anyone. She would regret wasting her first on me after waiting so long. I'd be out the door before she could say good morning. Fuck's sake. Why am I even *thinking* about shagging her?

It's that lush mouth, those are porn-star lips and, yeah, I pressed my thumb against her lower lip when she was sleeping to see if it was as soft as it looked. It is. And I didn't miss the generous curves squeezed into a too-tight white blouse and black trousers. *Stop thinking with your dick.* She's got trouble written all over her. I know her wedding is today, everyone knows, so what the fuck is she doing here dressed like that?

Her list of sins is long and growing. She broke into my mate's houseboat, got pissed on my tequila, slept in my bed, puked, and ate my Cocoa Puffs. That was my last box! I ordered it online before I left on this trip (I got hooked on them during my first US tour). You can't find them on Villroy or in nearby France. Believe me, I've tried. I mean, can I get chocolate cereal in France? Yes. Is it as good as Cocoa Puffs, the original and the best? No. Half the box was wasted on the floor. It's sacrilege, that's what it is.

"Well?" she asks. "Will you hire me? I could use the job and I do enjoy travel." So proper, so posh. She seems to have forgotten servants should be more deferential. Maybe even throw a sir in there.

I close the distance between us and pluck the wig off her head. "I know who you are, Your Highness."

Her face falls. "Oh." She looks up at me, her brows scrunched together in apparent confusion. "What gave me away?"

"Um, everything?"

Her lips form a sexy pout before she crosses her arms. "I know who you are too."

"Brilliant. We both know who we are. What will it take to get you off my boat? I need to get out of here before everyone looking for you turns up." I've been anchored here for two weeks, until her wedding today attracted the paps and press I've been avoiding after my latest scandal. I was pissed on too much whiskey this last time, but that didn't exactly help my case when the press turned on me. I might have said fuck the prime minister and the president of the United States for their part in bleeding musicians dry. I had to blame someone and they're at the top of the chain. I may have let slip some flabby phallic name-calling. "Limp sausage that no one would ever stick in their mouth" rings a bell. I was on a roll. It was probably the most creative I'd been in a year. But the bad press hurt the band and put the pressure on for the next album—which is due to the label very soon—to win back the public. I never want to hurt my bandmates, John and Max. We've all been through enough losing Charlie.

It was decided by those with my best interests in mind (those who get a cut of my money) that I should lie low until the next album is ready to release. I'm the songwriter of the group whether or not I've got an ounce of interest or creativity left in me. Officially, I'm on a meditation retreat in Tibet. Cruising around on a houseboat solo, going where I please when I please, is as close to meditation as I'm going to get. In any case, once the cameras went up toward the palace for Emma's wedding, I ventured out for one last meal before moving on.

She pinches the bridge of her nose and closes her eyes, seeming deep in thought. I'll heave her overboard if I have to.

She drops her hand, and her big hazel eyes light up. "Kidnap me. I'll pay you the ransom."

I back up a step. "Fuck no. I don't need that kind of attention." A certain amount of behaving badly is expected from a rock star—the groupies, partying, even brawling, all fine. Criminal activity? Too far. My days of petty crime are behind me. I don't know what's ahead of me. All I can see is a dark empty void.

Her voice comes out small. "I cannot go home. Not yet. Please let me stay. I'm sure I can be helpful in some way."

I don't know why she's running, and I don't care. She's a bloomin' princess. She can cash in one of her many jewels, like that huge rock on her finger, and find her own way out of here. Which is exactly what I tell her. She doesn't seem to hear me.

She lifts her chin and announces with a note of finality, "You, Jackson Walker, are exactly what I need."

I stiffen. She has some cocked-up notion that I'm going to play her knight in shining armor. Not bloody likely. I give her a scorching once-over from her full breasts to her narrow waist and generous curvy hips before meeting her eyes again. I'm not as immune to her as I'd like, my jeans tightening uncomfortably, but I bluster on. "Maybe you can pay me to stay on board another way." I lean close and her eyes widen, her lips parting as I stroke a finger over the rapidly beating pulse point in her throat. I lower my voice to a husky growl. "One month, no strings, and I own this proper princess body." Being a total dick, I'm expecting a slap and a quick retreat out the door. Which is my goal.

"Yes."

My jaw drops. "What?"

She beams at me, all sweetness, jubilant in her victory. "I'm all yours. One month."

I scowl. "No. That wasn't—"

She whirls and rushes to my bedroom. I hear the snick of the lock. I can't fucking believe this.

I stalk to the door and pound on it. "Open up."

"Not until we're at sea."

"I'm not keeping you here. That was meant to put you off."

Silence.

I head to the kitchen, rifling through the drawers for something to pick the lock with. I find a stiff bit of wire and go to work. A few moments later, the lock pops, and I open the door.

Her eyes are huge. "You picked that lock fast. Were you a criminal before you were a rock star?"

"Did I pick it faster than you?"

"Yes!"

I knew I locked the cabin. I want to ask where she learned that little trick, but my need to get her off the boat is stronger than my curiosity. Any minute, there's going to be a swarm of people and plenty of cameras. I don't want to make things any worse for myself or the band. "Now, Princess, are we doing this the easy way or the hard way?"

Her gaze drops to my crotch, and I nearly put my hand in front to cover. Cheeky. Her hazel eyes gleam. "The hard way."

I move fast, tossing her over my shoulder and pinning her kicking legs with one arm. I turn and head for the cabin door while her fists pummel my arse. *Ouch.* She can really throw a punch. "Stop pummeling my arse!"

I swat her arse.

"Ohh."

Was that a moan? I halt and then recover myself. "Hope you can swim." I head out the door and up the steps to the deck rail overlooking the sea.

Her hands fist in my shirt. "Don't toss me overboard! It'll create a spectacle! I've made a mess of everything and I can't face it yet!"

I hesitate at the raw emotion in her voice. I know about making a mess.

"Please, Jackson, I need some space to figure out next steps. And-and I want a taste of a different life. Mine is choking me."

I get that. The need for escape, the longing for something else.

She goes very still. "Please let me stay. I just need some time, some space, maybe reinvent myself. I'm so lost." Her voice cracks.

I blow out a breath, the words all too familiar. I want to reinvent myself too because me, right now, is nothing more than an empty shell of a man. The more I tell myself to get back to the music, the harder it is. I used to always riff and bounce ideas off Charlie, and now there is no Charlie. I haven't touched my guitar in months. I'm miserable, stuck, bloody finished. This whole houseboat trip is about finding the music again.

I haven't been the same since I lost Charlie. His death distorted the music into static noise. Fucking agony to lose them both. I've already got a year extension on my contract, but I have to produce the next album soon or I'm in breach. The record company can sue and will likely get the last asset I have, my house. I'm already low on funds after giving Charlie's four-year-old son and his ex-wife, Dorrie, a fat check to keep them off welfare. Dorrie's got enough to worry about with her severe asthma and taking care of an energetic boy. Charlie left them nothing; he spent it all on drugs and the lifestyle. I'm partly to blame. I'm the one that got him started with drugs. I got clean. He got worse. It's why his marriage fell apart. It's why *everything* fell apart.

I clench my jaw and set her on her feet. Up close, her eyes are green with a gold ring around the iris, big and hopeful, her cheeks flushed bright pink. It's like kicking a puppy. I can't do it. "I'm dropping you off at the next port," I grumble, going over to pull up the anchor.

She follows me. "In Italy?"

"France." It's only two hours away. Then I'll be done with her. She's a complication I don't need.

"I'd really prefer if you travel further afield."

I cock my head. "And I don't care what you prefer." I finish with the anchor and go above deck to the controls. My mate taught me how to operate the boat, and I took to it like a duck to water.

She's at my side a few minutes later as I'm pulling away from the dock. "I'll make myself indispensible to you.

Starting right now. Teach me how to drive this thing and then we can do it in shifts."

I grind my teeth. You don't *drive* a boat. Besides, this is supposed to be my solo trip so I can get my shit together, and I'm not babysitting her. "How about instead of being indispensible, you make yourself invisible?"

Her lower lip sticks out in a pout that I want to suck and bite. *No, no, no.* It hasn't been that long for me, has it? Since I got on the houseboat. A month. That's actually a long time for me, which makes me feel better. It's not her. Any pouty porn-star lips will do.

I turn my attention back to navigating away from Villroy.

"Thank you, Jackson. I promise you won't even know I'm here." She gives my arm a squeeze and it warms at the spot. Hell.

I let out a long low sigh. "Give your people a ring and let them know you're safe. I don't want them coming after me."

"Once we're well on our way, I promise."

I don't know why I think I can trust her promise after she's clearly capable of deception, hiding from her own wedding in disguise, but I do. She's something of a walking, talking contradiction.

A reluctant smile tugs at my lips.

∼

Emma

I secretly watch Jackson at the controls for a while, out of sight, in case there's some kind of boating emergency and he desperately needs me to take over. It looks pretty simple. Once we're out to open sea, he seems to just be standing there, so I decide to play maid. I do want to be useful.

First order of business—the messy bedroom. I pick the dirty clothes off the floor and look around for the laundry hamper. I find a tiny closet with one item—a guitar case. Well, I'm not going to pile dirty clothes on that. It's likely his prize possession. I set the dirty clothes on top of the dresser and start poking through the dresser drawers, looking for a laundry bag of some sort. There's only more clothes, none of them folded. Hmm, are these dirty or clean?

"What're you doing?"

I jump and whirl, my heart jackrabbitting against my rib cage. "I was putting away your dirty clothes."

"Why?"

"Because I'm indispensible." My voice rises at the end almost like a question. I add a curt nod to cement my assertion.

He grabs the pile of clothes from the top of the dresser and tosses them up to a small overhead alcove I now see is the keeper of the dirty clothes. He turns back to me. "Sit in the living room and don't touch my things."

Ungrateful. Doesn't he know it's an extraordinary gesture on my part to play maid? I have servants for this kind of thing. I open my mouth to say just that, but think better of it. It won't serve my goal of staying on the boat. I was hoping his threat of dropping me off at the next port was manly bluster, like my brothers do, but I have to consider the possibility that he meant it.

I head to the living room and take a seat on the sofa.

He follows and stops in front of me for a moment, staring at me with an unreadable expression.

"You should keep steering or we'll likely run aground," I tell him.

"Thanks for the tip, *Your Highness*," he grumbles and leaves.

Well. He needn't be so sarcastic. If he does allow me to stay, then our deal was that we'd be lovers, which I enthusiastically agreed to. What better way to break free from the old proper Emma than raw dirty sex with a bad-boy rock star? At least I assume that's the kind of sex he has. I haven't had sex in years. I'm long overdue and feeling just reckless enough to go through with it. I've already leaped from my old life. This brief reprieve is meant to give me a peek at a new life. I hope.

I head back to the bedroom and stare at the messy bed, considering what it'd be like to share it with Jackson. I flush with heat at the mere thought of him naked. It's a double bed, not very wide. I imagine he takes up most of it with his big muscular frame. I'll have to sleep pressed up against him all night. I rub the side of my neck, imagining him pressing a kiss there. I have never spent the night with a man. Sex, yes. Sleep over, no. It was impossible because of who I am and who he is. I wonder, not for the first time, how Adam is doing. It's been six years. Maybe he's married with a family of his own. A pang of longing jolts me into action, straightening the covers on the bed and smoothing them. It's not that I begrudge Adam any happiness. I just wish we could've stayed in touch. He gave me so much, taught me so much. For a time, I felt free, happy, like anything was possible. That was when I was young and stupid. Only eighteen, away from home for the first time at university. I had him for a year, and I loved him with all of my heart. Maybe that's the real reason I deserted Abdul. I felt nothing for him, not even the slightest bit of attraction, and I knew the difference.

I frown, looking at my handiwork. The bed doesn't look as good as when Lina does it. Maybe because there's no sham or decorative throw pillows. I pull the blanket over the pillows and tuck a bit, but now it doesn't quite reach the bottom of the bed. Ah, a compromise. I shift the pillows down, readjust the blanket to cover the bottom of the bed, and voila! Bed made nice and pretty.

I step out and peek into the tiny bathroom to see what I might be able to tidy up in there. It still smells a bit like sick. I quickly switch to breathing through my mouth and slide open the small rectangular window above the toilet. I turn my attention to the sink. There's some toothpaste bits and whiskers in there. My gut churns, bile rising due to the gross bits and the smell. I can't do it. I rush out of the bathroom and move on to the kitchen.

Okay, I can wash this little pile of dishes in the sink. I find a scrubber sponge and dish detergent under the sink and pour a generous amount of soap. A moment later, I realize my mistake. Too much soap. The bubbles are taking over, and everything is extremely slippery. No problem, I'll just run the water. *La-la-la.* I really am making myself indispensible. I run the sponge over everything, rinse for a very long time, and set it neatly on the counter.

I explore the rest of the cabin. The main living room doesn't have much. Just the U-shaped sofa and table, his closed laptop, and a built-in cabinet with a TV. I move on to the front of the boat with another smaller seating area similar to the living room, but done in a faded red. The matching curtains obscure the view. I lift the curtain and gaze at the sea. Freedom. It's a beautiful thing.

I sit there for a long time, staring at the horizon and then watching the coastline of France coming into view. It's not that far to Nantes, France. The yacht can make it in an hour. I'm not sure how fast this boat can go. I need to head off an abrupt departure. As in, Jackson makes me depart. He's not convinced yet that I could be a good travel companion. I could strip naked, but I'm unsure if he'd go for it or toss me into the sea. I fear I was more enthusiastic about a fling than he was. Then I remember how aggrieved he sounded about me spilling his Cocoa Puffs. He must really enjoy them. I'll make him some before we arrive at the port.

I go to the kitchen and dig around in the cabinet for a bowl before pouring a generous helping of Cocoa Puffs. The box feels really light. Only a few crumbs left at the bottom. Hardly worth even another bowl's worth. I pour them on top. Now for milk. The small refrigerator is pretty sparse. There's some take-out boxes, mustard, a bag of apples, Nutella, and eggs. Ah, there it is in the door.

I pour the milk on top, nearly overflowing the bowl. Now for a spoon.

Only a few minutes later, I've got everything I need and head up to where Jackson is at the controls. "I made you a snack."

He glances over and does a double take. "Did you dump the whole box in?"

I close the distance and hand it to him. "There wasn't much left. I'll buy you more."

He stares at it. "The milk."

"I thought that's how everyone took their cereal."

He closes his eyes and mutters, "The milk was sour."

"Why was it still in the refrigerator, then?"

His eyes lock on mine as he speaks through his teeth. "Because I hadn't taken out the rubbish yet. I wasn't expecting a visitor, yeah? Wasn't expecting a trespasser to annihilate my only supply of Cocoa Puffs."

A laugh escapes. He's so indignant over a children's cereal.

"You think that's funny?" he demands.

I back up a step. "No. I just saw something that was a little funny." I peek over his shoulder, pretending to be looking at something in the water. "It was a playful dolphin."

His eyes are slits of murderous intent.

My hand involuntarily goes to my throat.

"Your handbag is in the cabinet under the telly," he growls at me. "Ring home."

"I will. Is that how you knew who I was? You poked around in my bag? I would feel so much better if that was the case. Not that I want you to poke—"

"*Now*," he commands in a voice so full of authority I straighten my spine.

With as much dignity as possible, I turn and head back inside the cabin. I shouldn't have laughed. I'm really making a mess of things here. I don't think he's going to let me stick around for the servant thing or the lover thing. It's too bad because he fascinates me. He's wild and free, says what he wants, does what he wants. My good intentions toward him haven't quite panned out. Now that escape plans A and B are dead ends, I need a plan C. I love the idea of reinventing myself, of living a little and getting a taste of a different kind of life. It both gives me a reprieve from the mess back home and makes me hopeful for a chance at happiness. Of course, I will have to face the music eventually and beg forgiveness from everyone, especially Abdul. I cannot commit to a life with him. I know that now.

First, I need to call home. I retrieve my phone, settle in on the sofa, and pause. Who can I trust not to immediately drag me home and make me answer for my crimes? I'll call Anna. She's the one who supplied me with the getaway car, which means she's on my side. I connect with my maid, Lina, first and ask her to quietly find Anna and get her to the phone. Long minutes later, Anna says, "Just tell me if you're safe."

"I'm safe."

She lets out an audible breath. "Where are you? When are you coming back? What do you want me to tell Abdul?" That was a lot more than just tell me if you're safe.

"I'm with a friend on his houseboat."

"You're with a guy?" Her voice lowers. "Is this your secret lover?"

"No!"

"Well, I don't know. You surprised me running away like that. I thought you'd go for a brief car ride way before then, come to your senses, and quietly call the whole thing off."

I swallow hard. "In hindsight—"

She laughs. "Always twenty-twenty in hindsight. Welp, it wasn't the best way to go about it, but at least you stood up for what you needed. By the way, the servants found your gown in the laundry and the broken cake topper. Seems pretty ominous that your head snapped clean off."

"I thought so too," I murmur.

"Where's the car you took?"

"I parked it in the servants' lot. The keys are in the ignition."

"Well done, you! Who would've thought proper Emma could be so sneaky?"

"Well, you never know what you're capable of in a do-or-die moment." I smooth my hair. "It was rather rash."

"Understatement. Listen, I'm one hundred percent behind

you. I wasn't feeling this arranged-marriage thing, but, Emma, the press are camped out here and won't leave. The reports so far are not good for our family's reputation. Gabriel is furious that you left us to deal with the fallout, as is your mother, and Abdul's family refuses to leave until you follow through."

"I'm so sorry! I panicked!"

"There's more."

I grip the phone tighter. "What?"

"Abdul's family say if you don't return and marry him, they'll sue our family for breach of contract. There is signed paperwork. He could've married someone else years earlier, but he waited for you to reach twenty-five. He's fulfilled his end of the bargain. They demand that you fulfill yours. Honestly, I think they just don't want to face the public humiliation. If we could find some way to make it easier for them to step away…"

"I don't know what that would be."

"Me either. We have to think of something. They can't stay here indefinitely."

I let out a shaky breath. "I need some time away to think. I almost wish I could do what Polly did, you know? Get a fresh start as someone else." Anna is a distant cousin of Polly, the princess in hiding, who I'm finding very inspiring at the moment.

"You want to hide for a bit. That's okay as long as you know eventually you have to face your life."

"I know. I'm just…" My voice cracks. "I lost Father; I feel like I lost Mother; somewhere along the way I lost myself too. I just need the space to discover who I am away from the palace."

"Oh, sweetie, I understand. Let me think on it and I'll get back to you with a plan. I can probably buy you a week. I want you to enjoy some freedom too. You of all people need it the most. You've been much too rigid, like the old Gabriel. Maybe you just need to spend some time with someone more like me to loosen you up. Too bad I can't get away right now with my passion project—"

"Thank you, anyway. I'll think more on it too." Anna means well, but she pushes too much. I fear she'd turn me into a version of herself—brash and outspoken. Sometimes she comes off as extremely ill-mannered.

"Listen, I promised your mother I'd let her know when you got in touch. Expect a call from her shortly."

Heart in my throat, I numbly murmur my goodbye. Then I wait, staring at my phone, my entire body vibrating with tension. Long minutes tick by. My gut knots, my breath accelerating as my mind flashes to worst-case scenarios—she'll disown me; she'll exile me from Villroy forever. Just when I think I've been given a reprieve, the phone rings and I jump.

I grab it and check the screen. It's her private line. "Hello, Mother."

"What were you thinking?" she asks sharply.

"I'm so sorry for running away. I should've spoken up before I got to the point of panic, but I was so caught up in doing my duty, forming an alliance for the kingdom, making you proud, that I pushed down all my worries, and then they just erupted at the last moment."

Silence. I break out into a cold sweat, waiting for the hammer to fall. On my head.

"Mother?"

Her voice is ice. "You embarrassed our family, harmed our alliances not just with Abdul's kingdom, but with his allies, and, worst of all, you broke your promise. You brought dishonor and shame to the Rourke name. I never thought you of all my children would betray me in this way."

I suck in air. "It was not a betrayal. I agree it was inappropriate, and I'm so very sorry for the embarrassment."

"Sometimes apologies are not enough." The line goes dead.

I swallow hard, my eyes hot. I've spent my entire life attempting to meet her high expectations, an exercise in futility. I swipe at an errant tear. Maybe I don't want to try anymore.

I am no longer my mother's daughter, no longer a fiancée, no longer a proper princess. It begs the question—

Who is Emma Rourke?

4

————

Emma

If Jackson drops me off at the next port, where will I go? Could I travel solo incognito and explore a bit? Maybe by train. The weather is turning cooler now that it's November. I consider France, Spain, Italy, all familiar to me. I speak all three languages. I have an ear for languages. God, I'm tired. I rest my head on my arms and give my poor brain a break. It's been a crazy day.

My phone rings a few minutes later. It's a private palace number. It could be Anna. It could also be my mother with a final kiss-off or Gabriel ready to read me the riot act. "Hello?" I answer softly, as if that will soften the person's outrage on the other end.

"It's Anna. Okay. I've got a couple of possibilities. Adrian can get you a room at the Fairmont Monte Carlo. He's such a frequent spender at the casino, they always accommodate him. He says you wouldn't even have to leave the hotel. They have everything you could want, restaurant, spa, casino. Hey, now I want to go! What do you think?"

Adrian is my younger brother and an accomplished poker player. My chin quivers. He's supporting me despite the mess I've made. I take a calming breath, trying to think it through. I'm sure he's well known at the casino, which means I will be recognized, and my chances of a quiet retreat at a casino are slim.

"Sounds busy. What was the other possibility?"

"A villa on Lake Como, Italy. Lucas knows the owner, an A-list movie star, he won't tell me who, but he says it's only used in the summer. The only issue is, it's kind of isolated. Do you think a friend would be willing to go with you? Or maybe we could send Lina? I don't think you should be alone right now. You need the support of a friend. And you'll need guards. It's not safe, especially with the press's interest in your bridal flight. That's what I've been calling it privately to the family to make the point about you spreading your wings."

"I suppose that's as good a metaphor as any." It's twisted, but I kind of like it. I consider who I could ask to go with me to the villa. I have a handful of friends from other noble families. They wouldn't understand needing a break from royal life. They adore it. And my maid, Lina, would only remind me of home.

"I'll invite my friend along who owns this boat. His name is Jack." I go with a shortened version of his name, not wanting to share too much. He must've wanted privacy if he was taking a long trip solo. I doubt he'll want to accompany me, but it will make my family feel better to think I'm not alone. Actually, I *don't* want to be alone. I will do my best to get Jackson to consider it. The prospect sounds much easier than making myself useful on a boat.

"Ooh, Jack. I like the sound of that. Last name? How did you meet? Where's he from?"

"We met at a charity event."

A beat passes before she exclaims, "That's it?"

"Yes. He's looking for privacy."

"Sorry, Emma, that's not gonna fly. I had to push Gabriel hard to get you this week. He was frantic over your disappearance and, once he knew you were safe, furious that you left this mess behind."

"I'm sorry. I truly am. If I could do it over—"

"I know, but the fact is Gabriel could order you back here and you would be forced to obey your king. I am the only thing standing between your freedom and your duty. I want you to have this time, but there's a lot we're dealing with back here, and we need to know what you're doing and who you're doing it with. We can't manage the message with more surprises coming at us. You understand that, right?"

I hold the phone close and whisper, "It's Jackson Walker from Ignite."

She gasps. "Oh my God."

"He's been most kind during this whole, um, unexpected—"

"Emma, do you have any idea the scandal following him around right now? Do you know how bad it would be to have you associated with him? All of *your* scandal on top of his?"

"I haven't been following his press—"

"Well, it's *bad*. The press turned on him. A lot of his fans are speaking out against him. He insulted the British prime minister and the US president. He went too far. Oh, geez. And now we've got Abdul's kingdom and his allies turning against us. I'm sorry, Emma, and I say this as a *huge* fan of Jackson as a musician, but he's the worst person for you to spend time with right now. And do you have any idea of his reputation with women? It's worse than Phillip's! Manwhore to the extreme." Phillip is my older brother, formerly known as the royal hottie, with a rutting reputation to match. He's redeemed himself through his dedication to his fiancée, Ruby.

This new information only makes me think Jackson is the perfect person to hide out with for the week. If he's like Phillip, then I do understand part of him at least (commitment issues), and he would understand like no other person in the world the kind of scandal I'm embroiled in. He would want to keep things quiet, same as me. "I'm not worried about his reputation or his scandal. We would lie low.

Besides, Jackson and I are just friends." Sort of. I'm not sure if he finds me quite as fascinating as I find him.

She makes a derisive noise. "That is not the way he plays. How long do you think that friend thing would last alone at a villa? And he is not the kind of man you could ever bring home. Nobody would approve of him." She sighs. "I can only do so much."

My gut knots, a sour taste in my mouth. I've already disappointed my family with the Abdul fiasco. I don't want to risk disappointing them again. Obviously, I cannot get any romantic notions in my head where Jackson is concerned.

Anna goes on in a gentle tone. "You're not thinking straight right now, so I will do it for you. No to Jackson Walker. I'm sending you two guards and one of your brothers. And I know a brother is not your first choice as support, but, unfortunately, your sister is due back at work and leaving for the US soon, and I'm busy with everything here. It's the best way to keep this quiet. You get a one-week reprieve to get your head together, and then you have to return home and deal with your life."

I tense. She's sending me a babysitter. This is just like my old restrictive life. Everything chosen for me, my duty to my family and the kingdom overriding any of what I want. I don't even know what I truly want beyond a chance to discover who I am away from the palace. Maybe then my true desires will finally be clear to me and I'll have a chance at happiness.

I keep my voice level. "It's not even a sure thing that Jackson would accompany me, but I'd like to ask him. I will accept the guards. No brothers."

She lets out a long sigh. "Don't make me play the queen card."

Everything in me rebels. I hate feeling like I have no control over my life. I've had only the briefest taste of freedom, and the walls are closing in on me again.

"I love you, Emma. Please take what I'm offering."

My breath hitches. She loves me? My sister-in-law is still a newcomer to the family. But then I think of how she tried to talk to me about Abdul before the wedding day, how she was the only one who gave me an option to get away and think, and now she's the only one offering me a chance to breathe. It must be true.

My vision blurs with tears, my throat tight. "It means so much to have you on my side, Anna. I-I hope we can spend more time together when I return."

"I would love that. So you're good with the conditions?"

"Yes." It's my only choice. And she has done more than I could hope for.

"Great. Now where are you?"

"I'm heading for the port in Nantes."

"You know, I told Gabriel to look for you in Nantes. It's closest to Villroy, but no-o-o, he insisted that was too obvious and you'd either head up to England or down to Spain. The man was crazed with worry and obviously not thinking clearly. The rest of your brothers were no help at all. They were rooting for you not to marry Abdul and figured you were still on the island, hiding out somewhere. Gabriel and I knew you'd finally snapped and would leave Villroy."

I allow myself a small smile. My brothers might tease too much, but they do want what's best for me, and they knew that wasn't Abdul.

Anna goes on. "Silvia's upset you didn't turn to her. She would've taken you back with her to the US for a long visit." My younger sister by two years, Silvia, married an American and lives there now.

I stop smiling. Silvia and I haven't been close. She's Adrian's twin and they were glued at the hip for most of our childhood. She was always jealous of the bond I shared with Mother. "I wouldn't have wanted to intrude on her and her husband. I will touch base though."

"The jet's in Nantes since Phillip just flew in for your wedding. I'll let them know to expect you. Do you need anything? Clothes? Cash? Passport?"

"I've got everything I need." Not exactly true, but I figure

I can buy clothes in Italy. I don't want her to go to any trouble. "Thank you, Anna. I owe you."

"And don't think I won't collect!" She laughs. "I hope this week is just what you need. Bye."

I tell her goodbye and sit there for a moment lost in thought. I hope a week away will bring some clarity, though I know nothing will lessen the severity of the consequences I must face when I return. I'm not sure how to fix things with Abdul and his family.

The cabin door opens and Jackson steps inside. "We're here." He looks wary, like I'm going to insist on staying on the boat. I suppose I did give him a bit of a fight before.

I stand. "Right. Thank you for the ride. Will you be staying in Nantes or heading south?" I'm guessing he's heading toward warmer climates since it's November.

He runs a hand through his hair. "The weather's not looking promising on the Bay of Biscay. I might have to hold tight for a few days." That's by Spain.

"So, you're going to travel solo around Spain, the South of France, and finally get to Italy? Or was it China?" I smile brightly, letting him know I don't hold a grudge over his earlier brush-off. "That could take a long time."

He shrugs one shoulder. "I've got nothing but time."

"It sounds exhausting."

"I'll take breaks."

I step closer. "I'm taking a break too. I'm heading to a friend's villa on Lake Como in Italy. I've been granted a one-week reprieve from my life by the queen. Then I have to deal with the mess I've left behind."

"What'd you do? Run away at the altar?"

I grimace. "It wasn't quite at the altar, but, yes, I ran away on my wedding day. At least Abdul didn't have the humiliation of standing at the altar waiting for me. Not that it's much of a consolation." I push down the wretched feeling of regret. I should've handled this so much better, and now it's too late. "I will deal with it. The press, the mucked-up alliance, my former fiancé, my family's damaged reputation." *My mother.*

"That's a long list to deal with," he says in a surprisingly sympathetic voice. "Sounds like the world is against you. I know a bit about that."

I nearly hug him. I knew he would understand my situation. I so wish it were him accompanying me on this trip instead of my brother. I don't even know which brother Anna will send. I just hope it isn't Lucas. He's more likely to tease and harass than act as a confidant.

He turns, looks out the cabin window, and then yanks the curtains closed across them. "The press is lined up on the dock. How did they know you were going to be here?"

I worry my lower lip. "Maybe they're here for you."

He plants his hands on his hips. "Nope. No one knows I'm on this boat. And I borrowed it from my mate, someone I know from way back before I was famous, so no direct ties to me."

I let out a shaky breath. "They're probably here because my sister-in-law had to send word to get the jet ready at the private airport nearby for my trip to Lake Como." I take him in for a long lingering moment. He's a primal beast of a man with his growly voice, raw sexuality, and loose-limbed masculine movements. I usually only meet buttoned-up, clean-shaven, meticulously neat men. He tossed me over his shoulder and patted my bottom. And I liked it. I bite my lower lip, heart pounding, butterflies dancing in my stomach. I cannot do this. Can I? I'm already in so much trouble. But if I don't do something right now, then this is goodbye forever.

His gaze drops to my lips and jumps back to my eyes.

"Jackson, I so wish..."

"What?"

I shake my head. "I wanted to invite you to go with me to Lake Como, just for a week, but...I guess it was silly."

He closes the distance between us, his gaze searching my features. "Why do you want to be with me so much? Are you a fan?"

"God, no. Your music rubs my nerves raw."

He barks out a laugh. "I imagine you listen to classical music up at the palace."

"Among other things." I enjoy blues and folk music too, but I don't think a rock god like him would appreciate that.

"Just call one of your friends to join you. I'm sure you run in some elite social circles."

"Everything's different now," I blurt. "They won't understand why I want a break from royal life." And the truth is, I want everything he represents that I'm missing in my life. I know I'm not supposed to bring him with me to Italy, as per Anna, not that he wants to go, but maybe we could still have an…experience on the boat. It would be a huge step forward for me to experience the wild side that is Jackson, even if it's just one time. I have to make every moment count during the brief reprieve I've been granted.

I steel my nerves and say simply and honestly, "I don't want to say goodbye to you yet. I want you."

He takes a step back. "Wrong bloke."

I swallow hard, forcing a neutral expression. Clearly he doesn't want me back. It hurts, but at least I know. Now I can move forward, no regrets, where he's concerned at least.

I paste on a smile. "You didn't let me finish. I was going to say I want you to teach me guitar."

He gives me a skeptical look. "Right. Guitar."

"Perhaps you could recommend a similar colleague?"

"A similar colleague," he echoes.

I warm to the idea. It's not ideal, but it might be the only alternative. "Yes, someone equally edgy and improper. Maybe your colleague could teach me to play guitar."

His lips play at a smile. "I can't think of any similar colleagues. Employ yourself a music teacher."

I step closer and confide, "It's the improper part I need more urgently. They say you become like the people you surround yourself with. I've spent my life surrounded by proper people. I've got one week to experience a different sort of life. Part of the Emma reinvention program."

He stares at me for a long moment, and my hopes soar until he says, "You're barking mad."

I slam my hands on my hips. "Haven't you ever felt like you were going along happy as a clam, everything going the way you thought it should, and then you just wanted to leave it all behind and start fresh?"

He blinks at my outburst, but says nothing.

I look to the ceiling, willing my tears back. Maybe I'm fooling myself. Maybe I'll always be proper Emma Rourke, doing my duty, living the life laid out for me by others.

"Hey, don't cry."

"I'm not." I dash at a tear that escaped. "Forget it. My brother knows some Hollywood types. Maybe a male actor with low inhibitions would be willing to spend some time with me." I give him a watery smile. "I already know a low-inhibition female and she hasn't had much effect on me." Anna has been more of a curiosity than an influence, though she's growing on me.

He crosses his arms and growls, "And what do you plan on doing with this low-inhibition male?"

His outrage seems like a good sign. Maybe he does want me.

I lift my chin and say in a breezy confident tone, "I haven't decided what exactly I'd do with a low-inhibition male, but I know it would push me out of my comfort zone, and that is what I need. A shock to the system, something completely different."

He shakes his head. "You're just asking for trouble. Don't you have any sense of self-preservation?"

My back gets up because for the first time in my life I actually know what I want—him—and I can't have him. I pull out my phone. "As a matter of fact, I'll text Lucas right now. He's the one with the movie-star connections." I type a little note I have no intention of sending because I am bluffing like a champ. I would never go through my brother for help finding a man. After he finished laughing, he'd likely send a servant to fetch me home and hide me away.

I lift my head. "Lucas has already agreed to meet me at the villa with my choice of wild comedic actor, grunge drummer, or a rebel royal from Denmark. Wow, he is better connected than I realized. Decisions, decisions. Hmm, rebel or not, I don't need another royal, so the question is wild or grunge. What do you think?"

He snorts. "Bye, Emma."

Crap. That didn't work. I tuck my phone in my purse and say in an even tone, "Goodbye, Jackson." I gather what's left of my dignity and exit the boat. There's a black Mercedes waiting for me in the distance. I don't see my guards, but I know they must be here. They always ride with me. I hesitate, thinking I should wait for the guards, but I can't bear to go back inside after Jackson called my bluff. I've never propositioned a man before and the rejection stings.

The moment I reach the dock, the crowd swarms toward me, firing questions in rapid English and French. Cameras with zoom lens, handheld TV cameras, and cell phones follow my slow progress.

"Over here, Your Highness! Over here!"

"Why did you run?"

"Do you have a secret lover?"

"Was Abdul cheating on you?"

They press in on me, shoving microphones in my face. Camera flashes blind me. My heart races. I go on tiptoe, looking for the guards, and I'm jostled off balance. I can't find them. I should've swallowed my pride and gone back inside the cabin. I was so busy trying to make a dignified exit from Jackson I didn't realize the greater danger was out here. I've never had to push through the press on my own.

"Excuse me, pardon, I need to get through," I say and then repeat it in French. They close in so tightly I can't move. For the first time, I'm actually scared in a crowd. I shove my hands in my pockets, duck my head, and attempt again to move forward with no luck. A man grabs my arm, asking if a servant helped me escape. I jerk my arm out of his grip and bump into a tall man, another reporter. "Please! I need to get through!"

I lurch forward a step, jostled by shoulders and elbows. The volume of questions rises, but I can barely make them out with the roaring in my ears. Suddenly two men dressed in black head straight for me. It's Viktor and Oliver. I'm saved!

Viktor heads straight for me, and Oliver keeps going behind me. A hand lands on my shoulder and a fierce order rings out by my ear. "Back off!"

I whirl. That wasn't Oliver. "Jackson! You…" I trail off in horror as Oliver takes Jackson to the ground and stands over him threateningly.

I throw myself between Oliver and Jackson. "Don't hurt him! He's a friend of mine." I turn to Jackson, who's glaring at Oliver. I can feel it even through his sunglasses. "Are you okay?" He looks like he attempted a disguise, wearing a hoodie, cap, and sunglasses, but I recognized his voice. And his scruffy beard, nose, lips, hands—all recognizable to me. There isn't much I didn't notice about him earlier.

"Fine," he grumbles, getting to his feet. "That's what I get for playing knight in shining armor."

People close in on us, firing question after question, screaming both of our names, but Viktor and Oliver keep them from getting too close.

I impulsively grab him in a hug and beam a smile up at him. "You came for me."

He sighs so big it parts my hair. "You're a hazard to yourself."

5

———

Emma

Jackson and I are quickly hustled into the waiting Mercedes. The damage is done—someone recognized him after I said his name in surprise. There are pictures of us together and pictures of him flat on his back with a guard hovering menacingly over him. The only thing we can do is flee the scene.

The driver pulls into the street, and I breathe a sigh of relief. Viktor is in the front passenger seat and I'm in the backseat, sandwiched between Oliver and Jackson. I turn to Jackson. "Thank you for looking out for me. I've never been so scared in a crowd before."

He takes off his sunglasses and briefly meets my eyes before grumbling, "It was nothing."

"Ma'am, you should've waited for our approach," Viktor says. He's been with me the longest, a no-nonsense sort of man in his thirties with short dark brown hair, a square clean-shaven jaw, and a large intimidating build. I know I can trust him to be discreet in all things.

"I agree," I say. "I have no intention of repeating that mistake. So, should we drive around a bit, wait for the crowd to disperse, and then drop off Jackson—"

"Ma'am, this crowd isn't going anywhere," Viktor says. "They're waiting for Jackson to return to his boat."

"I'll get whatever you need from the boat," Oliver says to Jackson, "once you're safely on the jet." Oliver is newer to the family, so I can only hope he's been trained for discretion. His blond hair is buzz cut, which makes his face look more angular and stern, though he's probably only a few years older than me.

I glance at Jackson, who looks grim. I don't want him to feel forced into anything just because he tried to help me. "The jet can take you wherever you'd like to go," I tell him. "We can arrange for your boat to meet you there."

He slouches down in his seat, his eyes at half-mast. "I'm your guitar teacher, so I'm going with you."

My jaw drops, my heart pounding. Anna said no to Jackson Walker. His scandal plus my scandal is too much. Do I dare risk the wrath of my family? On the other hand, my family is already furious with me, and now that the press has put Jackson and me together, I'm knee-deep in the trouble I was supposed to avoid. It cannot possibly get any worse. Why shouldn't I grab this opportunity?

"Wonderful," I tell Jackson, working to sound casual. I cannot believe this is really happening. I'm spending the week with a legendary bad boy. That has to change a person. In the most delicious way. At the very least, I'll get guitar lessons from a master.

"Right," he says.

Oliver reaches across me and holds his palm out to Jackson. "Need the boat keys. I'll pack your things, deliver them to the jet, and then I'll have your boat moved to the port in Villroy."

Jackson straightens. "Why can't I leave the boat here?"

"No permit. No security."

"It's not of interest to anyone. It's an old houseboat."

"They know it's yours now, sir. Keys."

"It's the safest place for it," I tell Jackson.

Jackson blows out a breath, giving me an uneasy sideways look. Maybe he doesn't like the idea of having to return to Villroy with all the attention that will bring, but it would be much worse to leave the boat here unattended.

He digs the keys out of his pocket and drops them in Oliver's hand. "Just pack everything in the dresser, my toiletries, my laptop, and my guitar. Guitar is in the wardrobe." He slouches down in his seat and puts his sunglasses back on.

I can't help my smile.

∾

Jackson

I'm not planning to shag Emma. That's not what this is about. When she spoke from the heart, her eyes shining with tears, her voice raw and real, asking me if I know what it's like to realize you're stuck and need a fresh start, well, she got to me. That is my life in a nutshell. And not gonna lie, the idea of her asking some random guy to rub his improper *whatever* off on her rang alarm bells. Christ. She's too damn innocent to know what she's inviting. I would've stayed away with just a lingering sense of being a shit for letting it happen, but then she walked into a mob of paps and press like a lamb to the slaughter. They took advantage of her vulnerability and nearly trampled her in the process. I *had* to take action. Unfortunately, so did her guard. Why the hell didn't she wait for her guards to escort her? She needs a keeper. Ironic that it's me, a washed-up musician with my own scandal to live down.

She might be more of a mess than I am, and somehow that makes me feel better to find someone else in the same fucked-up place. I don't know. Maybe I'm just sick of being alone. Maybe I don't know what the fuck I want. I know what I don't want—more long days and nights trying to draw blood from stone. I'm under contract and have to return to the studio in January to lay down the next album. It's now mid-November. If I don't produce, I don't get paid my next advance *and* I get sued for breach of contract. And if I go belly up, there's no more money for Charlie's son, Jack. He's named after me. How could I not look after him?

I can feel Emma's tension as she looks out the window at the passing scenery on the way to the airport. She's anxious to make her escape, far from the judgment of others. I get that. Her vulnerability sucked me in. I'm probably going to regret this. I'm going away with a now infamous princess, and my only escape, my boat, will be near her home, which will definitely not go unnoticed. I'll probably have to face a mob when I turn up there next week. I should be fucking knighted for this. For real.

So we'll do the friend thing. I don't do relationships. And I definitely don't do virgin princesses. It'll be entertaining, though, watching this prim and proper princess attempt to be a rebel. She'll probably think it's wild just to play a song with a swear word in it.

I straighten out of my slouch and try to stretch my legs in the backseat.

Emma beams at me, her face lighting up. "I'm so looking forward to learning guitar."

My muscles relax. It's been a while since someone looked so happy just to be with me. I've pissed off a lot of people recently. "Yeah? And what will you teach me?"

She worries her luscious lower lip. "I could teach you languages, etiquette, ballroom dance, take your pick."

"Hmm, such a difficult decision with all these enticing choices."

"I studied philosophy at university, if that's more to your liking."

I lean my head back against the headrest and close my eyes, suddenly tired. I haven't been sleeping well. "Right then, as your new guitar teacher, your first lesson is to listen more than you talk."

"Because it will sharpen my sense of hearing, tuning me into the frequencies of voices and ambient background?"

I nearly laugh. Like I would ever in a million years come up with that. "Yeah."

She shuts up, presumably listening to ambient background. She's quiet the rest of the way, and I doze for a bit.

When the car arrives at the airport, she says, "I heard you breathing a lot."

"I do that. Almost every day."

"Also, the sounds of the car—the tires, the motor, the wind."

I have no idea what to say. That wasn't a real lesson. She looks at me expectantly.

"Brilliant," I say, and she beams an incandescent smile at me. Warmth steals through my chest. I don't deserve that smile. Truth is, despite my fame, she's slumming it with me. My family would be the servants polishing her shoes. My father left when I was two, and we were on welfare, even with my mum working a crap housekeeping job. I was expelled from grammar school for fighting, embarrassing my shy mum. People say I take after my shit of a father, which is why I never wanted a wife or kids. No reason to pass that along. My older brother was the star student, the favorite. Once I discovered the guitar, I calmed down with the fighting for the most part.

But Emma here is part of the elite. If I never hit it big with Ignite, we never would've met. She wouldn't have *wanted* to meet me. But then I remember Emma doesn't like my music. She couldn't care less that I'm part of Ignite. She doesn't want anything from me besides guitar lessons. That makes me relax a little.

The driver turns to us. "Would you like to wait for Jackson's luggage on the jet or inside the terminal, Your Highness?"

"We'll wait on the jet," Emma says. She turns to me. "The terminal is very small, just a few rows of vinyl seats. I think the jet would be more comfortable. Or we could wait outside if you prefer."

"I'd like to stretch my legs," I say.

She nods once. "Then I will do the same."

She says a cordial thank-you and goodbye to the driver and Oliver before stepping out of the car. I join her, and Viktor appears at her other side.

The car heads back the way it came. I'm really doing this. Oliver will return with my stuff and then I'll be off to live with a princess for a week. I glance at Emma. She's huddled against the cold, her arms crossed tightly across her middle. She ran away from her wedding without stopping for a coat, probably in a complete panic. I'm sure she'll have hell to pay when she returns home. I'm about to offer my hoodie when Viktor takes off his black blazer and settles it over her shoulders.

"Thank you," she says, pulling it close around her.

Viktor looks impervious to the cold in a black T-shirt with black jeans. "You're welcome, ma'am. There's a small service road over there for your walk."

"Sounds good," she says, and the three of us head over to the narrow road.

Viktor is a silent presence, and Emma has gone uncharacteristically quiet. I have no interest in small talk, so I just walk. Surprisingly, it's a comfortable silence, and the view of an empty field actually feels peaceful.

After our walk, we return and board the jet to wait for my luggage. I let Emma go ahead of me as we climb the stairs to the jet's open door.

Emma stops short just as we step inside and mutters, "Lucas," like a curse.

I take off my shades and stick them in the collar of my shirt. A tall bloke in his twenties with dark brown hair and a matching beard lifts a hand in greeting from one of the seating areas farther back with tables. Prince Lucas Rourke.

He grins. "I volunteered for Emma duty since it was my friend's villa. And I believe the proper greeting is hello, wonderful brother of mine, thank you for saving my ass and giving me this wonderful escape from my personal catastrophe."

Emma marches forward, and they have a heated discussion. I glance around, no other royal family here. Just the pilot and a flight attendant at the front of the jet, both of them smiling, seeming entertained by the Rourke siblings.

There's four rows of wide reclining seats up front. I take off my hoodie and cap before taking a seat by a window in the second row. Viktor is already sitting in the first row.

"Can I get you a drink, sir?" the flight attendant, a voluptuous brunette in her twenties, asks.

"Water, please." It arrives a moment later. "Thanks."

She lingers and says in a low husky voice, "I'm a big fan."

"Thanks."

"How did you meet Emma, if you don't mind me asking?"

"I do mind, actually."

She bobs her head, turns, and goes back to her post near the cockpit.

I unscrew the cap of my bottled water and lift it to my lips when Emma plops down next to me, bumping my arm. Water spills onto my beard and shirt.

"Sorry!" she exclaims, wiping my beard with her fingers. "Soft," she says in a breathy voice. "So wet."

I'm both turned on and amused. "Could I get a napkin?"

The flight attendant rushes over with a handful of napkins. I wipe my beard with a few, and Emma wipes my chest, scrubbing hard enough to make the napkin rip.

I brush her hand away. "I'm good, luv. Stand down with the napkin."

She looks at the shredded napkin in disgust. "What a poor product."

The flight attendant quickly takes our rubbish and brings us both fresh bottled waters. Emma smiles at the flight attendant. "Thank you, Peggy."

"You're quite welcome, Your Highness." Peggy gives me a speculative look, like she wants to say more, but then the pilot calls her for the preflight check.

"Please just ignore my brother," Emma says tightly. "This

is going to be wonderful." She leans close and whispers, "I'm so glad you agreed to join me."

I whisper back, "Was the sultan a total wanker?" That's her former groom.

She flushes pink. "He wasn't a sultan yet, and he was perfectly nice."

"So why'd you ditch him?"

"It just felt wrong," she whispers, her gaze downcast. "My gut instinct told me not to go through with it."

"Did it feel right all the way up to your wedding day?"

She frowns. "No."

"So what took you so long to dump the guy?"

She folds her hands primly in her lap. "I don't wish to discuss it."

A large hand appears in front of me followed by the unsmiling face of her brother. "Hello, I'm Emma's brother Lucas."

Emma shoves at him. "Go back to your seat."

He ignores her and says to me in a tone heavy in disapproval, "I know you."

"I don't think we've met," I reply. He knows my rep; he doesn't know me.

His blue-green eyes narrow into slits of displeasure, all aimed at me. "I'll be with you the whole time in Italy. Consider me your chaperone."

"Lucas!" Emma hisses. "Go away!"

I offer Lucas an easy smile. "Nice to meet you, chaperone. Emma and I are just friends."

He regards me suspiciously before taking the seat directly across the aisle, buckling in, and glaring at me.

And now it's a party. The three of us plus two guards in a villa for the week. Brilliant. Is it too late to bail out?

Emma turns to me, speaking in a low fierce tone. "He's letting us into the villa and that's it."

I keep my voice low. "Does he know that?"

"Yes," she whispers. "I told him as much. I don't buy that he volunteered. Gabriel—that's my older brother, the new king—sent him to babysit me. I'm twenty-five years old, but Gabriel still sees me as a little girl with pigtails. He has no *idea* what I'm capable of."

I stare at her, intrigued. "What're you capable of?"

She lifts her chin. "Lots of things."

"Like philosophy?"

She glares at me. "It's bad enough my brothers tease me. I don't need it from you."

I grin. "But I never had a little sister to tease."

Her lips twitch. "No excuse."

I chuckle despite Lucas's eyes boring into the side of my head.

"And, yes, I know about philosophy, but also useful things."

"What kind of useful things? Picking locks?"

She smiles mysteriously. "Among other things. My brothers underestimate me."

I glance over at Lucas, and he makes a few hand gestures, pointing to me and then Emma. Jesus. The message is clear—finger through the hole, slash across the neck, and a jab in my direction. His brows lower, his gaze murderous. Message received—shag my sister and I kill you.

I face front. "So Lucas is one of those overprotective big brothers?"

"No, that's Gabriel. Lucas is just a pest."

"I see." I can feel him watching us. I keep my voice low. "No shagging expectations on this trip, right?"

She blushes bright pink, her fingers pulling at her collar. "N-no. I would never expect…" She coughs. "I don't know why you would say that. I mean, you did say before…but then…let's not talk about…" She clears her throat. "Okay?"

I can't help teasing her. She can barely spit out the words after claiming she needed edgy. "What about—" I cough "—pushing you out of your, um—" I clear my throat "—comfort zone?"

She narrows her eyes before saying primly, "There are other sides to a woman besides her unmentionables."

I'm dying to hear her say an unmentionable part. "What don't we mention?"

"Shut it."

I laugh.

~

Emma

I am furious. Not because of Jackson. I'm used to teasing from the men in my life. It's Lucas. Bad enough he's here, but does he have to stare at me and Jackson like we're an exhibit at the zoo the entire trip to Italy? It's embarrassing and terribly obvious. I don't think he knows Anna warned me not to bring Jackson, because he hasn't mentioned it, and she probably didn't say a word about it, assuming I would've abided by her conditions, which I'd normally do, but one thing led to another, and now it's done. Clearly, Lucas knows Jackson by his scandalous reputation. I'm not sure if Jackson and I are plastered all over the internet yet, and I don't want to know. I'd really hoped to get to know Jackson a bit on the flight, but after Lucas interrupted our conversation several times, Jackson slouched down in his seat and pulled his cap over his face.

I do appreciate Lucas providing a safe getaway place for me. I just thought I'd be able to...let my hair down and explore whatever there is to explore within me, away from palace life. Lucas reminds me of home and family and duty. Not that he ever seems hampered by it. Maybe because he was the third-born boy. No pressure to learn how to lead as king, and my parents gave my brothers lots of freedom. Lucas isn't what I'd call wild, or, if he is, he's very discreet about it because you almost never hear salacious things in the press about him. He loves to party, though, mixing it up with A-listers, and lets loose easily. I sigh. Maybe I should try to be more like Lucas, except I don't enjoy big noisy parties with inebriated people, and I go to bed promptly at nine thirty, which is before most parties start. I've followed a strict routine for years, telling myself the rules and high standards I set were necessary to carry on my role representing Rourke royalty. Now I'm at a loss.

We land at the Milan airport, where a car is waiting for us. Lucas gestures to a large wheeled suitcase that's brought out of the jet's cargo area. "Silvia packed some of your things for you."

My cheeks flush with shame, my throat thick. Silvia is my one and only sister, whom I didn't confide my worries to. I should've turned to her. We're blood. And she still made this thoughtful gesture for me. "That was very sweet of her."

Lucas inclines his head. "I'm curious what she packed you. She was pissed off that you were so unhappy and she never heard a peep about it. Maybe it's full of old-lady clothes. Oh, wait, that's just your regular wardrobe. Ha-ha."

Jackson laughs, and my brother immediately frowns.

I glare at both men, even though Lucas is right. My wardrobe consists mostly of modest pastel dresses ending at the knees. Nothing remotely sexy. I don't know why I thought I had any chance of seducing Jackson into liberating me from my old proper lifestyle. Even if I had a flattering dress, he's supremely uninterested in me other than in a teasing big-brother way. Plus we have an obnoxious chaperone. I suppress a sigh. I will learn guitar and get some breathing room on this trip. That's it. I must be grateful for what I've been given and hope that this time offers some clarity for my future.

A rented black Mercedes with tinted windows is waiting for us. Oliver claims the driver's seat. Lucas insists Jackson take the front passenger seat so he can stretch out his legs, even though Lucas also has long legs. He's only an inch or so shorter than Jackson. I slip into the backseat with Viktor, and Lucas takes his seat with us a moment later, looking smug.

He turns to me. "The villa is very safe, remote, and equipped with a state-of-the-art security system. There's a caretaker, who will stop in daily to see to our needs."

"That sounds wonderful," I say with as much enthusiasm

as I can muster given his behavior toward Jackson. "Thank you," I add belatedly.

"Finally, a thank-you," Lucas crows.

I grit my teeth and say nothing more. It's dark now. Today has been the never-ending day, and I can't wait to go to bed.

Once the car is in motion, Lucas pulls out his phone, texting rapidly, probably reporting back home that we've arrived safely.

I close my eyes, nearly dozing off, when it hits me that Lucas could've mentioned that Jackson was with us. Crap. I know the guards and staff would never report back on my behavior unless I was in danger. Lucas is the weak link. Or it could be that Jackson and I are already plastered all over the internet. I do *not* want Gabriel issuing a royal command that forces me home. I must obey my king. I'm about to ask Lucas what he was texting about when he turns to me and slowly shakes his head, his mouth drawn in a flat line.

My stomach drops. It's over. My nails bite into my palms. The simplest thing, bringing a guest of my choice, and it's gone.

Lucas whispers directly in my ear, "I just found out Anna told you not to bring *him*."

I nod.

"Gabriel is not happy."

I grimace. "Is he forcing me home?" I whisper.

"I don't know. Anna says she's dealing with him. But, Emma, the press is—"

"Don't tell me. Please."

His gaze is direct, his tone sharp. "We'll talk later."

My eyes widen at his tone. He's never sharp with me. He's always warm and easygoing. Great. On top of everything else, now I'm going to get a lecture from the party guy.

It's all too much. I close my eyes, shutting out the world, and doze off within minutes.

I wake to my brother nudging my arm. "We're here."

I step out of the car. The house is dark, so I can't make out much. It's a large multistory stone home right on the lakeshore. There's some beachfront area, a pool with a smaller stone structure, and a patio.

The guards stick close to me as I trail Lucas with my luggage. Jackson follows behind. He's probably regretting coming to my rescue and getting roped into this. Well, good news, Jackson, this will likely all be over tomorrow at the king's command. Lucas does the security code for us by the front door and steps inside.

"Oh, how lovely," I murmur, heading for the living room. It's warm and cozy with stone walls and post and beam ceilings. The two plush beige sofas with red throw pillows and rustic-looking wood end tables and coffee table look so inviting. It's so different from home, and I love it already. The floor is brick. It's an open floor plan, the dining room just off to the side with a long wide-planked wooden table with chairs that have wicker seats.

I turn to Lucas. "Whose place is this? It's so wonderfully rustic."

"Blaze Tanner. And you don't have to worry about him popping in for a visit. His wife just had twins and they'll be in LA for a while."

"Oh, I love his movies."

Jackson remains quiet.

I turn to Lucas. "Thank you for your help today. Will you be heading back to Milan tonight or leaving in the morning?" I attempt to tamp down the urgency in my voice, knowing I might only get one night of freedom and don't want an unnecessary chaperone.

"Let's talk." He inclines his head toward the living room. "You too, Jackson. By the way, big fan of Ignite."

Jackson shoves his hands in his pockets. "Thanks."

Lucas takes a seat on the sofa and gestures us over. "Come on, I don't bite. Much."

I take the seat next to him, and Jackson remains standing by the dining room.

Lucas cups his hand by his mouth. "I'll have to yell for you to hear me."

"It seems like a family discussion," Jackson says.

"Actually it concerns you too!" Lucas shouts, exaggerating the distance between us.

Jackson ambles closer, but doesn't join us on the sofa.

Lucas leans forward, elbows on his knees, and meets my eyes. "What's going on with you, Emma? I've never seen you act like this before. You were always so by the book. Running away from your wedding to be with a rock star?"

"I had nothing to do with this," Jackson barks. "Leave me out of it."

I immediately jump to Jackson's defense. "I hid on Jackson's houseboat, a complete coincidence, and then, after he very kindly agreed to drop me off in Nantes, he came to my rescue when the press and paparazzi mobbed me."

"Where were the guards?" Lucas demands, looking around accusingly.

I glance around. Viktor and Oliver must be scouting the house and property. "It wasn't their fault. I ventured out before I saw them. They were on their way to me."

"Why would you do that?" Lucas asks.

I shrug, careful not to look in Jackson's direction. I don't want to share the real reason—Jackson's rejection—in front of him. I'd like to keep a shred of dignity.

"Why?" Lucas presses.

I blow out a breath. "I wasn't thinking clearly. This has been the longest day of my life."

His voice gentles, and somehow that makes the words slice deeper. "Gabriel was frantic over where you went. Abdul was crushed. He waited so long for you. And his family is furious. And surely you know about Jackson's latest scandal. Now he's tied to you in the press."

"Fuck the press," Jackson says.

Lucas glares at him and says in a voice of steel, "Our family's name is being dragged through the mud." I've never heard my brother take charge in this way. Maybe because he's never had the opportunity, being third in line for the throne. I just wish I wasn't the one he's decided he's in charge of.

"I don't love Abdul," I say softly. "I'm not ready for marriage."

Lucas's aquamarine eyes, so like our father's, are kind and understanding. "You cracked under the pressure. It's a wonder you didn't crack earlier the way you always rigidly stuck to royal protocol. You're as bad as Gabriel."

I nod. "That's why I'm so grateful for this brief reprieve in Italy."

He pulls me in for a quick hug and kisses the top of my head. I give him a watery smile at the unexpected affection.

"Get some sleep," he says. "You'll need it to face whatever is coming at you tomorrow."

I straighten in my seat. He's right. I don't know what tomorrow will bring, but I know it won't be good. I've made more of a mess of things bringing Jackson here, and Gabriel is sure to let me know his displeasure. Tonight might be my only night of peace for a long while.

Lucas stands and asks Jackson, "Why exactly are you here?"

Jackson lifts his palms. "I'm—"

I leap from my seat. "Jackson has agreed to be my guitar teacher."

Jackson rubs the back of his neck while Lucas looks at him suspiciously.

"Isn't that nice?" Lucas drawls. "Guitar lessons from a rock star. New part-time gig for the front man of Ignite?"

"I'll go first thing in the morning," Jackson mutters.

"No!" I exclaim. Lucas's head whips toward me. I'm usually not prone to outbursts and rarely raise my voice. "You're staying," I add in a level voice.

Lucas shakes his head. "Emma, you have *no idea* the heads that will roll with him here with you. Abdul and his family, our family, the press, especially with our new venture—"

"It's one week," I say in as reasonable a voice as I can muster. Though it might only be one day.

Jackson grumbles, "I'm off to bed." He grabs his duffel bag and guitar case and heads upstairs.

I follow him, dragging my heavy suitcase up the stairs. Lucas snatches my suitcase and carries it for me, passing me on the stairs. Once he gets to the top, he tells Jackson, "Here's your room." He points to the room closest to the stairwell. "Come on, Emma, you get the master bedroom as your reward for finally pulling your head out of the sand and taking charge of your life. Even though you did it in the most disastrous way possible. See what a good big brother I am?"

I open my mouth and then close it again. It almost sounded like a thank-you was in order, but I'm also vaguely insulted. He deposits my suitcase in the room and steps in the hallway, announcing loud enough for Jackson and the entire country to hear, "I'll be in the room next to Emma's."

The door to Jackson's room shuts.

I turn to Lucas, mortified. "What is your problem? I don't need you to stand guard. Jackson is no threat to me."

"Emma, Emma, Emma, your innocence will be your downfall. Don't you know his reputation with women? He will use you and drop you without a backward glance." He shakes his head. "Guitar lessons. *Please.* He's trying to seduce you."

"The guitar lessons were my idea! And he's not even interested in me. He treats me like an annoying little sister, teasing and whatnot."

"That's how it starts. He's disarming you and then bam! He's a manwhore, and I mean that in the uncomplimentary way."

"How could that ever sound like a compliment?"

He leans close. "Listen, you're in way over your head. I don't know how you possibly became friends with him—"

"We met at a charity event. His band was playing there and I was the emcee."

"And then what? You kept in touch?"

"No. But fate intervened and landed me on his boat."

"Fate." He snorts. "Wake up! He wants a royal trophy, nail the princess. He was probably just waiting for you to leave your fiancé—"

"It was nothing like that!" I cross my arms and lift my chin. "And stop lecturing me. I can handle myself."

His voice gentles. "You've been engaged since you were sixteen. You have so little experience with men of any kind, let alone his kind. I'm worried about you."

I uncross my arms, softening with his real concern. "Don't worry, okay? I promise I know what I'm doing. I just need a break to learn guitar and breathe." I grimace. "For however long that is."

He leans down and kisses my cheek. "I understand. I enjoy breathing too."

I laugh a little.

"And I'll be here as long as he is."

"Lucas!"

He turns and goes into the bedroom next door. Argh!

6

____

Emma

I'm eager to get my pajamas and toothbrush out, so the first thing I do is haul the large suitcase onto the extremely comfortable-looking king-sized bed. I unzip it and find a folded note on top of my neatly packed clothes.

Emma,

I know you're a couple of inches shorter than me, but I couldn't bear to send a rebel bride off with your sad collection of wannabe Mother dresses. Did you let her pick out your entire wardrobe? Hope my contribution to the cause fits. Anna threw in one of her favorite dresses she can't wear anymore "due to the cleavage factor." Tough to be the queen. Ha. She says it barely covers her ass, so it should be knee-length on you.

Love,

Silvia

P.S. Please visit me in the US. I miss my big sister.

Gah. What is with the waterworks? I wipe my leaky eyes. Just because I made one impulsive spontaneous decision suddenly I'm losing control of my emotions. I was raised to be stoic, to keep messy feelings buried deep inside. Already some of that is loosening up for me. I should be glad, but it's more uncomfortable than I thought it would be.

I sniffle and wipe my nose with the back of my hand. Maybe trying to break free of my strict constraints means I'll completely lose control, and everything will pour out of me. Next thing you know I'll be touchy-feely, spontaneously hugging everyone like my sister-in-law, Anna, does. It's already happening! I impulsively hugged Jackson when he showed up on the dock to save me from that mob of people. This isn't who I thought I would be. I wanted to be happy, but in control of myself.

I head to the en suite bathroom, grab a tissue, and blow my nose. One look in the mirror at my watery eyes and drawn expression has me straightening my spine. Rourke women are not soft.

I march back to the suitcase and get to work, pulling out the things I need. Then I can't help but peek at the new things Silvia packed. I set my modest pastel long-sleeved dresses on the bed and pull out Silvia's contribution—black skinny jeans and a red V-neck sweater. Not cashmere, but it's soft. It's a very American-looking outfit. I guess that makes sense since she's been living there for years now. For shoes, I have my usual sensible flats in black, navy, and taupe. Anna sent me a dark green dress with a plunging neckline, cinched waist, and short skirt. It's made of some soft clingy material. Do I dare wear a dress like this? Well, I did want a fresh start. Tomorrow. Now I need sleep.

I hang the dresses in the walk-in closet, get ready for bed, and conk out the moment my head hits the pillow. I spring out of bed at my usual time, five thirty a.m. Would I like to be one of those people who can sleep in? Yes, I would. The problem is, no matter what time I go to bed, I'm up at five thirty like I have an internal alarm clock. This is why I stick to a strict nine-thirty p.m. bedtime.

Today is my fresh start. I will seize the moment before anyone shows up to say differently. I'm not sure which of my two new outfits to go with, so I try them both on. First, the jeans. Ugh. I can't get them past my hips. I'm shorter and curvier than Silvia. The sweater fits at least, but with no jeans to wear them with or trousers, I take it off again. I pull on the dark green dress from Anna. Wow. I am popping out of the top. Can you even wear a bra with this thing? The skirt ends mid-thigh on me, which means it must've been scandalously high on my five-foot-nine sister-in-law. I'm five feet three. Do I dare wear it? Will my brother laugh at me? More importantly, will Jackson like it?

I think of Jackson sleeping down the hall, used to beautiful sexually confident women throwing themselves at him. Then I think of stupid Lucas next door acting like a Victorian-era chaperone. Lucas can deal with me trying a few new things. And I will smack him if he laughs.

I put the dress back on the hanger, grab my large toiletry case, and head for the shower. Silvia did a good job, even packing all of my favorite makeup, creams, and perfume. Maybe my maid assisted her. The simple kindness touches me deeply.

An hour later, I'm completely ready, wearing the dark green dress with the only bra that could possibly be worn with the plunging neckline. It's lace with rather open cups. I can't go braless or I'll be flopping all over the place. I'm eager to get started on what might be my one and only guitar lesson. Maybe it will lead to more in the quiet privacy of Jackson's bedroom. It's do-or-die time. I have never been so brazen in my life sneaking into a man's bedroom, but I've got nothing to lose. I slip my feet into my taupe flats, open my bedroom door as quietly as possible, and stealthily make my way down the hall to Jackson's room. My brother's door is still shut. He's never been an early riser.

I quietly open Jackson's door and slip inside, shutting it behind me. He's sprawled on his stomach on a queen-sized bed, the white comforter covering only his bottom half. He's shirtless, his tanned muscular inked back exposed. I tiptoe closer, and my mouth goes dry. The tattoo centers on a jagged ring on his upper back with flames blazing up and across his shoulder blades. I'm dying to trace the flames with my finger, but don't dare.

His face is turned away from me, so I walk around to the other side of the bed. "Jackson?"

No response.

I nudge his shoulder. "Jackson."

He grumbles something unintelligible.

"Can you give me a guitar lesson before Lucas wakes up? I don't want him as a witness. I'm sure I won't be very good as a beginner." I'm quite pleased with my reasoning. It doesn't sound at all like I'm hoping for more than a lesson.

His eyes are closed. "What?"

"I don't want Lucas to watch me learning guitar. Can we do it now?"

"Do what?"

"Guitar."

He cracks one eye open. "What time is it?"

I glance at the digital clock on the nightstand. Six thirty-five. "Nearly seven."

His eyes close. "In the morning?"

"Yes, of course in the morning. Did you think you slept the day away?"

He puts a pillow over his head.

I take it off. "Don't do that. You need oxygen."

He groans. "Lock the door. Don't want Lucas barging in giving me hell."

I freeze, my heart pounding. *Lock the door?* Does that mean he's on board? Is he naked under that comforter? Did he see my slutty dress and get the idea that I'm looking for sex? This is all so much easier than I anticipated.

I rush to the door and lock it and then rush back to the bed, kick off my flats, and slide under the covers, breathless. This is definitely stepping out of my comfort zone. And it has been so very long, much longer than I'd ever admit to him. After my relationship with Adam, I resolved to save myself for Abdul. I was technically engaged to him and thought it unfair to be seen on the prowl with other men. Not that I've ever prowled. I've been a proper princess my whole life except for the Adam year, and finally I can break free.

I snuggle closer, his body giving off heat like a furnace. It's wonderfully toasty and he smells so good, like the sea and musky male. Except he's not moving. Did he fall back asleep already? His face is turned the other way. I lean over him to check. His eyes are closed, lips parted, his breathing deep.

I flop back on the mattress next to him. He wasn't tempted enough to resist the pull of sleep. I sigh. At least he didn't kick me out. Maybe he thought that would take too much time away from his sleep and it was easier to let me stay. Or maybe he thought I'd raise a fuss and it would draw Lucas or the guards to my rescue. I did give him a fight before on the boat.

I slowly lift the cover and peek at him. Not naked. Dark blue boxer briefs. Maybe when he wakes up, he'll be ready to do something. I roll to my side toward him and put a hand on his back. He sleeps right through it. I can relax since he's back in a deep sleep.

"I do like some of your music," I whisper. "The ballads. What you played at the benefit, your big hit 'Inferno,' was discordant to my ears. I don't know how to explain it. Some music moves me deeply. It can lift me up, sometimes to an ecstatic spiritual experience. I've been brought to tears too, not that I actually cried. I just felt them threatening."

I stroke up his back and over his shoulder blade, loving the warmth and the play of muscle under my palm. "I listen to music all the time. I love the energy of live performances and attend as many as I can. When I'm not listening to music, I hear it in my head. I haven't played my flute since I left home for university. I'd like to bring music back into my life again. That's why I asked you for the lessons. I do enjoy acoustic guitar. Electric would be okay, too, if it wasn't too loud."

I withdraw my hand and pull the covers up over his

shoulders and mine. Then I just lie there with my eyes closed and drift, my mind replaying the events of the past twenty-four hours. I'd felt stuck. Why hadn't I spoken up sooner? I suppose it was the way I was raised—duty, honor, obligation. Always the kingdom, the family, above self. Gabriel followed the same dictates, and I liked being part of that illustrious lofty way of life. He, along with my mother, the former queen, were my role models and are deeply embedded in the fabric of who I am.

"I never really explored what makes me happy," I whisper to a sleeping Jackson. "I'm not sure I even know. Besides the occasional music that moves me. But I can't spend my whole life just listening to music. I need to do something."

I get quiet, trying to think of what that might be. What are my strengths? I know self-defense and how to pick a lock thanks to Adam. And I'm fluent in French, Spanish, Italian, and Mandarin Chinese. I was working on Malay for my new life in Kainei with Abdul, but it wasn't gelling. Maybe that was a sign that I didn't want to continue down the path set out for me. I lie there, staring at the back of Jackson's head. His dirty-blond hair is messy and sticking up near the top. I find it endearing. I smooth down the messy hair, sigh, and roll to my back, staring at the ceiling, wide awake.

A very long time later, Jackson turns his head toward me and opens his eyes. "Hey."

"Hello."

He sits up and swings his legs over the side of the mattress away from me. My shoulders droop. All this time cuddled next to him and sharing to his unconscious self made me feel kind of close to him. I thought when he said lock the door earlier he ultimately wanted some intimacy.

"Do you find me tempting?" I ask softly.

He rests his elbows on his knees. "Emma," he says on a sigh.

"Do you?"

He looks over his shoulder at me. "I find all women tempting. Nothing personal."

I huff and scramble out of bed.

"Did I insult you?" Not waiting for an answer, he heads for the en suite bathroom.

"No," I tell his retreating back. "I was just curious. Now that that's out of the way, we can start guitar lessons."

"Wait there." The bathroom door shuts.

I wait so long it's ridiculous. It sounds like he's taking a shower. A vision of a naked, wet Jackson fills my mind vividly. His damp hair slicked back, the hard planes of his chest. He's hung, I'm sure of it. In my vision he is. Thick and hard because of me. Because I've tempted him more than any other woman he's ever seen. Heat pools low in my belly as I imagine my lips on that gorgeous body, his scent, his taste.

Eep! I jump as the bathroom door pops open suddenly, steam billowing out.

He has a white towel wrapped around his waist, his hair slicked back just like in my lusty fantasy. He rubs a hand over his beard. "When I said wait there, I didn't mean literally in that spot. Why don't you get my guitar and strum it a bit, get comfortable with it, yeah?"

"Oh, sure, and you'll just be..." My gaze follows his amble to his duffel bag in search of clothes.

He tosses the bag on the bed. "Having a cuppa." He grins.

I smile at his playfulness. It's almost flirty, though I shouldn't read too much into it. He did say he likes all women. I turn away, worrying my lower lip and telling myself to stop hoping so much. But this is the new me, reaching out for what I want, and the fact is I'm here and all those other women are not. I allow myself the pleasure of staring at his wide bare chest, the light dusting of hair, the lines and grooves of muscle, the bulge of his briefs.

"Guitar is right behind you," he prompts.

My cheeks flush with heat. I take the hint, turning to the guitar case propped in the corner next to the closet. I lower it to the floor and open it, my ears tuned in to the rustle of clothes as he dresses, my imagination filling in the magnificent details. The rustling stops a few moments later, so I assume he's done. I pull out a glossy acoustic guitar with black inky designs drawn over the face of it, swirls and starbursts. This guitar has been well loved. I'm actually a little surprised he's letting me handle it by myself. I carefully remove it from its case and bring it with me, taking a seat on the cushioned bench next to the foot of the bed.

He joins me there, wearing a gray T-shirt with ripped jeans, feet bare. He smells delicious, like soap and something distinctly him, so masculine and sexy. "Here, let me tune it."

I watch as he plucks different notes, strumming a few chords and adjusting the knobs on the back.

He hands it to me. "Are you right-handed?"

"Yes."

"Okay, so the way you're holding it is good. Is that comfortable?"

"Very." It's not exactly, but I'm just honored to be holding his prize possession.

"Loosen up your wrist." He points at it. "Start with a scale. Easy." He demonstrates with an air guitar, plucking strings. "G, A, B, C, D, E, F, G."

My brain can't make the connection, so I hand him the guitar. "Here, you do it and then I'll try to imitate. I need to see it on the real thing."

"Maybe I should pull up some YouTube videos."

"I'm here for *you*. You're the expert, not some random stranger on the internet."

He shakes his head. "I'm not an expert."

"Come on, I've been waiting all morning for this." I glance over at the clock. "It's nearly nine o'clock!"

"What time did you get in here again?"

"Not that long ago," I fib. "Now play." I try to hand him the guitar, but he won't take it.

"I'm not some trained monkey you can order around."

"I know. You're a rock god."

His jaw clenches. "Not anymore."

"You're a trained musician," I say through my teeth.

"Self-taught."

"Are you going to teach me or not?" I burst out. Oops. I hope I didn't wake Lucas.

He stares at my cleavage. "Did you nick that dress from the woman who lives here?"

I glance down to see my lace cups showing a bit. I adjust the dress and meet his heated eyes. My body flushes with heat in response, my nerve endings crackling to life. "I'm not a criminal."

"You broke into my houseboat."

"That was part of a clandestine escape. It doesn't indicate a life of crime. This dress was a gift from Queen Anna."

His voice is rough. "It suits you."

I smooth my hair in its neat chignon. "Thank you." I turn to the guitar and pluck a few strings. There's some dots on the neck of the guitar, so I press those with my other hand. A bunch of sounds come out, but it's not the scale. He reaches around and adjusts my fingers, saying the notes as I pluck them. My pulse thrums through me, heat flashing through every part of me all the way up to my scalp. God, I hope he can't tell.

He drops his hands. "Do it a few times, saying the notes."

I can concentrate a lot better when he's not touching me. I run through the scale, forgetting halfway, and he corrects me. It doesn't take long until I can hear when it's right.

"Now I'll show you a couple of chords."

I like those. They sound like real music. "Do you have any sheet music? I can read music. I used to play flute when I was younger."

"No. We should get you some, find some easy songs you'd like to learn." He thinks we have all week. I fear we only have this morning now that word has gotten back to Anna and Gabriel that Jackson is here with me.

"Can you teach me something simple right now?"

He's quiet, staring at the guitar. Just when I think he's going to refuse, he takes the guitar from me. "This is Bob

Dylan's version of 'House of the Rising Sun.'" He plays for me, his eyes closing as he sings along in his deep gravelly voice.

The hair on the back of my neck rises, goose bumps breaking out over my skin. It's beautiful and moving, his voice deeply resonant.

He finishes and opens his eyes, his expression more relaxed than I've seen since we met. "That song was originally an old English folk song about prostitution, which made it extra exciting to fifteen-year-old me." He gives me a lopsided grin that squeezes my heart. "It was the first song I ever played."

"It was wonderful!" He hands me the guitar and tells me the chords. I start slowly, his agile fingers helping me along. I manage to get through the first verse.

"Good," he says. "Now sing along." He recites the lyrics for me.

I play again, concentrating on my fingering, humming along, too embarrassed to sing in front of him.

"It's more fun if you sing it too," he says, and repeats the lyrics for me.

"I can't sing."

"Everyone can sing. I'll sing with you. Go ahead."

I start playing again, the notes coming a little easier, and his deep voice joins in. He nudges my shoulder and I hum a little, blushing, and stumble on the chord. I shake my head and start again, Jackson quietly watching me.

I stare at the guitar, pleased I can play a simple song.

"We'll work up to singing, yeah? No judgment."

I lift my head, smiling, and hand him his guitar. "Thank you, Jackson, for everything. For coming here with me, for teaching me, for putting up with my brother. It means a lot to me."

"Thanks for inviting me." He stares at his guitar. "This is the first time I've played my guitar in four months."

"Why haven't you?"

"I couldn't. I tried, and I don't know." He traces a finger

over the inked swirl on the front. "I just lost my drive, my passion for it."

"Keep playing."

I stand and slip out of the room, hoping he'll continue in privacy.

I stop in the hallway, listening. A few moments later, I hear him strumming "House of the Rising Sun" and singing along quietly. *Yes.* I break out into a wide smile, tipping my head up, my eyes closed, letting the music wash over me, lifting me up.

7

Jackson

I open the refrigerator in search of breakfast, pumped from my guitar lesson with Emma. It's early for me, but I'm ultra-awake. The buzz of discovering music like it was way back in the beginning through teaching her caught me by surprise. This simple lesson made all the pressure of creating something great or original disappear. Hearing her hesitant notes gain in confidence, her self-conscious humming, that beginner's eagerness just opened up something in me. I never thought of teaching before, but passing on the gift of music to an eager student blew my mind.

I find some eggs and milk, a loaf of bread, and make myself toast and eggs. Pretty much the limit of my culinary talent. This place was stocked for us ahead of time, which is really cool. I don't even mind Lucas being suspicious of my intentions. He should be, with my rep. There's no shortage of women on the road, but I gave up on groupies after Charlie died. I gave up most of my vices then cold turkey—no groupies, no cigs, no weed. I cleaned up because he became a cautionary tale. Fucking hell, I miss him. He'd been with me since I first picked up guitar at fifteen and we formed a band. He would've got a kick out of Emma, probably doing a killer impersonation of her posh accent.

After breakfast, I put on my boots and leather jacket and explore the grounds. It's an amazing view, looking out over the lake, hills in the distance. There's a built-in pool with a stone poolhouse, a stone patio with cushioned chairs and chaise lounges, along with scattered benches to take in the view. It's quiet here. The house is on a plot of land far from its neighbors. Fame steals your privacy, and money buys it back.

I take a seat on a bench facing the lake and stretch out my legs. I like being on land looking at the water better than the other way round. The houseboat was borrowed from a mate, who hasn't used it since his marriage three years ago. I wanted it for the privacy more than anything. But this private villa in Italy works even better. I've got more room, company if I want it, and a caretaker to deal with stuff.

"Mind if I join you?" a deep voice says from behind me.

I'm not surprised to see Lucas. I have a feeling now I'm going to get The Talk. "Yeah, man, have a seat."

"Never get tired of this view," he says, rubbing his hands together and blowing on them. It's a little cool and he's only wearing a light blue button-down shirt, no jacket. He must've rushed out here for the chance to speak with me alone. "You eat?"

"Yeah, I had something earlier."

He nods.

Silence except for the sound of the gently lapping water. I wait. The silence stretches so long, I'm beginning to think he just wanted to enjoy the view.

Finally, he speaks. "I'm thinking about heading to Milan, about an hour drive, you up for it?"

"Nah, I'll sit tight here."

"You sure?"

"Yeah, I don't want to be in the public eye right now."

"Maybe tomorrow. Mondays are pretty quiet around here. We could bring one of the guards to keep the press away."

"I'm good, thanks."

He drums his fingers on his leg. "It's so dead around here."

"I like the quiet."

"You're rock 'n roll, man! You seriously like the quiet?"

"I didn't used to. I burned out from all the touring and shite."

His gaze is hard and direct. "Tell me the real story about how you met my sister. I know she's not a fan. She likes blues music, folk, and classical."

My lips part in surprise. Emma has hidden depths. That's some deep stuff. My music is more visceral, raw. "We, um, met at a charity event like she said. She introduced my band. It was a coincidence that she landed on my boat."

"Be straight with me," he says urgently. "We're all worried about her. This runaway bride thing is so out of character for her. She's been a rule follower her entire life. She loves the rules, lives for them. Now she's flying without a net and hanging with you. Why are you here, Jackson? The truth."

I meet his eyes. "She invited me."

"Why would you say yes? Do you want her?"

"She needs a keeper."

"I'm her keeper!" he barks. "Our entire family is her keeper! Tell me why you're here!"

I rub my forehead. Emma wasn't kidding about the overprotective big-brother thing. "I won't hurt her. I'm just teaching her guitar."

"Bullshit!"

The words come tumbling out. "Listen, I'm here because I've been holed up on a houseboat for a month, trying and failing to pick up the damn guitar, and then Emma turns up and asks me to come here and teach her guitar. At first it was a no, but she ran into trouble with the press and paps, nearly getting trampled, so I intervened, and the only thing to do after that was run with it. All she wanted was a short break from the mess she made, and I get that because I need the same thing. So here I am."

"So you're just two lost souls looking for some peace?" he asks, heavy on the sarcasm.

I stare out at the lake. "You know I lost Charlie."

"I'm sorry," he says, his voice gentle. "Yes, I heard."

I swallow over the lump in my throat, staring off in the distance. "I haven't been the same since. I don't want to play Ignite's songs anymore; they remind me of him. I felt like Emma, just wanting to say fuck all this and start afresh, but I can't. I'm trapped in a contract. Have to produce new material. That was something Charlie and I used to do together. I riffed with him, bounced ideas off him. My creative well is dry; the passion that drove me dead and gone." I meet his eyes. "Today's guitar lesson with Emma was the first time I've been able to play guitar in months. I connected with music again. That's huge for me. Maybe she's doing more for me than I am for her with these lessons."

"So you don't want her?"

I keep a neutral expression, hiding the lust I've been trying to ignore since I found Emma sleeping in my bed back on the boat and she opened those big hazel eyes at me. "Nothing's going on. We're friends."

He stares at me so long I'm sure he's seen through me. Finally, he says, "She's been engaged since she was sixteen. She's been sheltered and bound to her royal duties her entire life. Do you understand? She's like a baby colt trying out her legs. Kid gloves, man."

Don't touch. "Got it."

He claps a hand on my shoulder. "Hurt her and you're dead."

"I have no intention of hurting her. I taught her the first song I learned earlier—" my voice gets hoarse, my throat tight "—and it felt like a weight off my chest, like I could breathe again. Music is alive in me through her. It's a revelation."

He stares at me for a long moment, taking my measure, before a wide smile stretches across his face. "She's your muse. Never piss off the muse."

A slow smile breaks out. Maybe she is. "Bloody right."

He stands. "All right then. I'm going to check if Emma wants to go into town. Maybe she can pick up something less old lady to wear. Have you seen her dresses?"

"Have you?"

He frowns. "What do you mean?"

I think back to earlier, the revealing green dress hugging her luscious curves. "She said it was a gift from Anna."

"Shit." He turns and heads back to the house.

I smile to myself. Emma is coming out of her cocoon, it seems, and I'm the lucky bastard who gets to witness it. I won't touch though. I know better than to mess with this fragile beginning between me and the muse. Music is beckoning me back to her, and I'll do everything I can to stay in her and Emma's good graces.

～

Emma

I'm on pins and needles all day, waiting for the phone to ring or for a car to pull up with Gabriel springing out of it to read me the riot act and escort me home.

Nothing.

No texts. No phone calls.

Anna must be running interference for me.

Lucas and Jackson are getting along now.

Peace.

Thank you.

～

Jackson

The next morning, the bedroom door creaks open and my eyes fly open. I've always been a light sleeper. I'm on my stomach, my head turned toward the door. It's Emma, backlit by the hallway, fully dressed, this time in a soft-looking jumper and jeans. The jumper clings to her magnificent tits. I close my eyes and imitate the sleep of the dead. She's an early riser. I bet she's here to beg for her next guitar lesson, and I'm too tired to move.

I hear her lock the door, tiptoe over to the bed, and the soft sound of her shoes coming off. She has no idea how tempting she is crawling into my bed in the early morning. Most guys would take advantage. She's lucky it's me, and I'm not interested in proper virgin princesses. I can appreciate her curves without touching. Though last night she didn't seem so proper. She binge-watched an Italian soap opera while eating crisps and snort-laughing at the screen. I witnessed her eating crisps right out of her cleavage. She was a mess and much more interesting than the telly, which I couldn't understand anyway.

I can feel her staring at me.

"Jackson?" she whispers.

I ignore her.

She slides a warm hand over my bare shoulder. "It's time for our guitar lesson. It's past seven this time. I know you like to sleep in."

I grumble and turn my head the other way. Sleeping in means noon or later. The covers lift and she slides in, pressing right up against me. Just like yesterday. She has no sense of self-preservation. She sighs, leans close, and strokes my back, her voice small and vulnerable. "My father died a few months ago."

My heart pumps harder at the dark despair I hear in her voice. I've never felt protective of anyone, yet I want to spare her that darkness.

Her hand leaves my back, and she settles on the bed, squeezing herself up against my side, confessing some more in a low voice. "I miss him terribly." Her voice catches. "My mother went into such a deep state of grief, I feel like I lost her too. We were always so close. She just shut down, holed up in her room. She'll barely speak to me and this was before I made a mess of everything. I've spent my whole life modeling myself after her regal example. I guess that's why I got the courage to leave my arranged marriage. She just seemed indifferent to my wedding and it didn't mean as much to me to try."

She would've married a guy just to please her mum? That's fucked up.

"Everything's different now back home with the new king and queen in charge, and maybe that means I need to be different too, you know?"

I keep to my fake sleeping silence. I don't want to embarrass her, and she seems to need to get it all out.

Her voice rises in volume. "I was my mother's pride and joy. After four sons, I was her much-wanted daughter. She had another child just to give me a sister. Turned out she had twins, a boy and a girl. The twins were close, and I was a third wheel."

She was still the favorite. Otherwise, why would she care so much what her mum thought about her life? My older brother was the favorite, and I long ago stopped caring what my mum thought of my life. She was relieved when I moved out.

She sighs. "Maybe I wasn't as close to my mother as I thought. She kept the seriousness of my father's condition from us until nearly the end." She shifts and then her hand lands on my back, her fingertip tracing my ink. It tickles a little, but I soldier through. "I've learned my duties well and to what purpose? Everything's changed. My parents no longer rule. The new queen, Anna, is completely revamping the palace, the entire island, actually, with her new ideas and industry. I don't belong there anymore." Her voice cracks. "I've lost my place."

I can't bear the misery in her voice. I shift my head toward her. "If you married that bloke, you would've had a new place."

She jackknifes upright. "Ahh!"

I sit up and cover her mouth with my hand. "Shh, Lucas will hear and storm the room."

Her eyes are huge. She pushes my hand away. "How much did you hear?"

"Everything."

Her jaw drops. "And you faked sleep to trick me into confessing all my most vulnerable truths?"

"You needed to talk, so I let you."

She flops down on the mattress and pulls the blanket over her head. "I'm so embarrassed."

"Nah. I quite liked it. You seemed like a real person."

She yanks the cover down. "As opposed to what? A robot doll?"

I bite back a grin. "Do those exist?"

"I'm glad you find me so entertaining."

I lie on my side and prop my head on my hand. "I find you fascinating."

"You do?" she asks softly.

"Hell yeah. You were the favorite child. I wasn't. Now I can hear what it was like on the other side."

"Were you bad?"

"Yeah, Princess, I was bad. A very naughty boy."

"I find that fascinating. You could teach me to be naughty."

I stifle a groan. Fuck's sake, she has no idea how tempting she is. I know better, I do. And I'm not getting tangled up with her overprotective brothers either, especially when one of them is a king.

"Should we just add the naughty stuff to the guitar lessons?" I drawl, playing it cool. I can play with her without crossing the line.

She rolls to her side, her big hazel eyes lighting up. "Yes."

My fingers tingle with the need to touch, to slide a hand into her soft-looking hair, draw her close—

I flop onto my back and stare at the ceiling. "I'm not so bad anymore. I've given up most of my vices."

"But you used to be bad. I saw pictures of you brawling outside a pub."

I turn my head toward her. "Right. I used to fight a lot

more. I've mellowed now at the ripe age of thirty. I don't have anything to prove to anyone. I made it to the top. And I'm not so angry now like when I was a kid."

"You grew out of it." She purses her lips. "It seems I should've met you several years earlier."

"I was a mess then. Much like yourself now, but with more alcohol, drugs, and women."

She sits up. "Now that you're awake, we can do another guitar lesson."

"Answer one question for me first."

She looks at me warily. "What?"

"Why were you a runaway bride?" Part of me thinks it was a fluke. A last minute case of cold feet and she'll go back to her old life. Maybe even marry the man chosen for her.

"I told you before, my gut said it wasn't right. I only agreed to the marriage to carry on tradition. My parents had an arranged marriage that turned to love. I don't know what flipped the switch in me, maybe it was just building inside me, but I suddenly had to escape, so I ran."

"So if everything went back to normal at the palace and you knew your place, would you marry the next man chosen for you?"

She slowly shakes her head. "Something in me broke. I'm not the old prim and proper Emma anymore. I just need to find out who the new one is. That's where you come in."

"How's that work?"

"Guitar lessons to start."

"And then what?"

"You teach me how to be bad."

I ignore my dirty mind raging with ideas. *Virgin princess here.* "You already throw a good punch."

She beams. "I do, don't I? I'm pretty handy with self-defense, including using a knife as a weapon."

I suppress my shock. "Was that part of your proper princess training?"

"No, silly, that was from...never mind." She scrambles out of bed and heads for my guitar. "Is it still tuned?"

My mind turns over what she said. Why would she know how to use a weapon? There are some unusual quirks to Emma. This is only the third day I've spent with her, and I'm getting sucked in. I have to put some distance between us. "You shouldn't come in here anymore."

"Why not?" She plucks a few notes on the guitar.

I stand by the foot of the bed about to snap that I don't want her here, but she's sitting there on the bench seat, cradling my guitar like she's in love with it. I remember that feeling when I first discovered guitar. I inherited it from an uncle I'd never met, my mother's brother. It was his prize possession and she returned from the funeral with it, offering it to me and my brother. I wanted it; he didn't. That was the beginning of my first and only love affair.

She looks up at me with her big innocent eyes. "I need this. Please keep teaching me in the morning. Lucas will ruin it with his judgmental looks. He'll tease me and laugh at me for being so terrible at it."

"Lucas will probably go out in the afternoon. He went to Milan yesterday."

"But I can't count on that. I can count on him sleeping in."

I sit next to her and she hands me the guitar. "Maybe I want to sleep in too."

"I did let you sleep."

"No, you talked my ear off." I tune the guitar, something in me settling down. Maybe it's me tuning in, back to what means something to me. I play a few notes of "One Thing," a ballad I wrote for Ignite, and then keep going, singing along. It doesn't hurt the way it normally does to play the song when it's just me playing for her.

When I finish, she exclaims, "Oh, Jackson, I got chills! That was so beautiful. Teach me that one."

So I do.

She fumbles the chords. It's a more advanced song. She's blushing, embarrassed over her missed notes. I stop her, my hand over hers. "Don't put a lot of pressure on yourself. It's

not about getting it right. Just…let your fingers play. Whatever sounds good to you, yeah?"

She does a scale. "That sounds good."

"Basic, but okay. What else?"

She holds up her fingers. "My fingers are getting sore.
Don't you have a pick?"

I retrieve one from the case. "You can use it, but it's better
to build some calluses by playing a lot."

"Calluses? That sounds terrible."

"But your music will sound good." I stand, walk around
to the bed, and flop back on the mattress, closing my
eyes. "Play."

She does her scale and each of the chords I taught her.
Then she's plucking randomly, strumming a few strings
before stopping abruptly. I can feel her staring at me.

"I know you're not sleeping," she says.

"I'm listening. Play 'House of the Rising Sun.'" I remind
her of the chords.

She does, slowly making her way through it. She's doing
pretty well for only her second lesson. She practiced yesterday. If she keeps it up, she'll get there really quick.

I sit up. "How about you take the guitar with you and
practice by yourself in the morning? You've got a good ear.
I'll teach you whenever Lucas goes out." Her climbing into
my bed every morning is trouble waiting to happen.

"No. This guitar belongs with you." She hands it back.

I let out an exaggerated sigh, keeping my tone light. I
don't want to squash her newfound joy in music, but one of
us has to draw the line. "Please tell me you're not going to be
here at dawn again tomorrow. I need my sleep."

She smiles cheekily. "If you don't want me here, then lock
your door." She whirls and sails out of the room.

I sit there for a moment wondering why she looks so
pleased with herself when it hits me—she'll just pick the lock.
I am never going to be able to keep her out of my bed. It's
going to be bloody torture to keep my hands to myself.

The twisted thing is how much I like it.

8

No one here but me and my borrowed guitar. And the guards, of course, but they're very unobtrusive. Oliver is stationed outside and Viktor is upstairs. After lunch, Lucas and Jackson went out for a ride among the hills on two motorcycles kept in the garage here. Lucas didn't want me on the back of a motorcycle for my own safety, and no amount of arguing on my part worked. Jackson looked like he found the whole thing amusing. It's not funny in the least to have over-protective older brothers. It's damn irritating. I smile to myself. I'm loosening up already, using more swear words in my head. It's only my second day here and I'm actually starting to relax.

I strum the guitar for a while, trying to just "play with it" the way Jackson said. It's tough to play willy-nilly with no sheet music in front of me. It doesn't sound good, the notes not gelling. I pull up some YouTube videos on my phone and watch some beginner guitar lessons. Then I search for sheet music online. I find a few pieces I like and try them out. It's slow going.

After I get tired of that, I explore the house. It's odd, but this is the most alone I've been in my life. At home, there's my family, servants, visitors, guards. At university, there were other students and Adam. I almost feel a little nervous, which is silly. There's a security system, and the guards are here.

Upstairs are four bedrooms, each with their own en suite bathroom. The master bedroom, where I'm staying, has the largest bed with an upholstered bright geometric-patterned headboard done in blue and green. Rustic post and beams on the ceiling in here, along with a few chairs for reading by the floral-draped windows. The other three bedrooms are clearly for guests, all done in a neutral white and tan color palette. I wave to Viktor through the open doorway of his room when he looks up from his phone. He gives me a curt nod.

I head downstairs, trailing through the living room and dining room. There's also a family room and kitchen, but I don't feel like watching TV or eating. I put on my white wool coat, another of Silvia's thoughtful items packed in my suitcase, and wander to the lake.

It's so quiet I can hear the distant sound of birds, the lapping of water, the rustle of the breeze. I shiver as the wind picks up, and turn back to the house.

It's too quiet in the house. So this is what total freedom feels like. Quiet and alone with my thoughts. It's rather boring.

I find a stereo system in a living room cabinet and turn it on. Jazz. I fiddle with the controls. It's some kind of streaming service offering different music styles. I'd normally stop on a mellow song, but I decide to search for rock. It lacks a good melody-harmony counterpart, but it has noise and energy. My nerves jangle as I hit upon just the right song, and I take that as a good sign. It's counter to my usual tastes.

I push the coffee table to the side, clearing some space, and do some experimental twirls. I glance around. There's only a high window on one wall of the living room and a large window on the other wall, overlooking grass and trees. Very private. I take the pins and band out of my usual neat chignon and run my fingers through my hair. Then I lift my hands in the air and swing my hair around. Woo! That felt good. I rock my hips experimentally, and then I let loose, dancing wildly all over the living room as the song builds to a crescendo. I jump on the sofa and play some air guitar, rocking my long hair back and forth to the beat.

The song ends and I lift my head. Another rocking song! I jump down and rock out some more. I'm pumped, exhilarated, moving like a woman possessed. I run my hands up and down my body. I am rocking these jeans. I found them in the dresser. They're sexy and tight. I experiment with some growls.

And then I step on the coffee table and ROAR!

I shift and roar to the east! To the south! To the west!

Then I leap off the table and dance like a crazy woman. No one can stop me. I'm out of control!

"Everything all right, ma'am?" Viktor asks, appearing out of nowhere and sounding very concerned.

I straighten abruptly and smooth my hair. "Yes, thank you. I was just dancing."

"It sounded like you were hurt, ma'am," he says, completely serious.

I will myself not to blush. "Well, I'm not. Thank you for your concern."

A ghost of a smile crosses his expression before he returns to his usual neutral expression, bows, and heads back upstairs.

Talk about killing the moment. I make a hasty retreat to my room for a shower.

I'm just finishing drying my hair when I hear a loud drumming sound right overhead. I go downstairs and look out the windows, going from room to room, trying to find the cause. Viktor is already downstairs, speaking in a low urgent voice through his wireless headset to Oliver outside. There it is, in the sky, a helicopter is coming in for a landing just behind the house. Who is it? Did the owners decide to stop by? Reporters? My heart slams into my chest at a horrifying thought. What if Abdul is here to kidnap me and take me back to his kingdom for a forced marriage? His monarchy has absolute power. He could've brought his guards with him. Anna said Abdul's family was still at the palace demanding I fulfill my obligation. Maybe he got tired of waiting.

I briefly debate hiding, grabbing a knife to assist in the fight, or approaching with a confident smile. I compromise by slipping into the kitchen within reach of a weapon and wait, barely breathing.

There's a knock at the door and then the doorbell chimes. Surely, if it was Abdul's people, they would just break down the door to get to me.

I quietly approach the front foyer and peek around the corner at the door. Viktor goes to answer it. I spy Gabriel in profile through the high window of the door, talking to someone, probably Anna. Two guards stand at attention behind him, along with Oliver. I hang my head. It's over. My week was only two days and now I must answer for my crimes. I won't even get to say goodbye to Jackson. He's still out with Lucas, and I don't even have his number.

I gird my loins and step forward as they enter. "Hello."

Gabriel glowers down at me, his aquamarine eyes sharp, his expression hard. Shades of our Viking ancestors are apparent in his big muscular build and stance. He's often said he was born in the wrong century and should've been a warrior king.

I'm about to blurt, "I'm sorry," when he grabs me in a crushing hug.

"Okay," Anna says with a laugh. "Let her breathe. I told you she was fine. Sorry, Emma, he had to see for himself."

I nod, the air squeezed out of me. Gabriel finally releases me. "Emma, why didn't you come to me? I would've freed you from your agreement with Abdul."

I lift one shoulder. "There was just so much planning, so much momentum pushing me forward, I didn't give myself permission to think of an alternative."

The three guards step inside, waiting nearby.

Gabriel studies me intently. Anna looks sympathetic.

I lower my voice. "I guess it just built to a crescendo in my mind and then I broke."

"Come home with us," Gabriel orders.

"Don't rush her," Anna says, giving his shoulder a squeeze. She turns and hugs me before drawing back, her hands on my shoulders, a knowing look in her brown eyes. "I hear you have a visitor."

I gulp. "Jackson helped me when I darted into a crowd of reporters before the guards were ready for me and—"

She cuts me off. "And then there were lots of reporters and paparazzi all over the pair of you, so you made a speedy getaway, and you thought it couldn't get worse, might as well invite him to stay. For guitar lessons, right? Because the two of you are just friends." There's not a trace of sarcasm in her voice, so I have to assume this is the story she's been telling Gabriel after Lucas filled her in on the pertinent details.

Gabriel's eyes bore into me.

I flush and focus on Anna, who I know is the key to me being here for as long as I have been. "Yes, that's exactly right. Thank you for understanding and for everything, really. I don't think I would've even taken the out if you hadn't had a car waiting for me, so thank you for that too."

She smiles. "See, Gabriel? I told you that was the right thing to do. I mean, I tried talking sense into her before that, but she's just like you, she gets an idea in her head and that's it."

His brows draw together in a scowl. "Just like me? You're the one who clings to an idea like a bulldog with a meaty bone."

"Maybe we both have that wonderful trait." She goes up on tiptoe and kisses him.

He softens, smiling.

The new king and queen of Villroy are young and in love. I wonder if this was what Villroy's leaders were like when my parents were young. Somehow I doubt it. Anna doesn't follow many of the prescribed rules, though she's doing her best to preserve traditions as she leads us forward. I have a newfound appreciation for Anna and her brash outspoken ways. She was the only one who saw my distress and did something about it. She cares.

"Cute outfit," she whispers to me.

"Thank you." I changed into a simple white silk blouse from my own things and a fresh pair of sexy jeans from the dresser. The woman who lived here left several pairs of jeans behind, probably because she was pregnant with twins and wore maternity clothes.

Gabriel strides into the living room, looking around. Their guards remain in the entryway and Viktor heads back upstairs. "Where's Lucas?"

"He went for a motorcycle ride with Jackson."

Gabriel shakes his head, his expression grim. "I sent Lucas to look after you. It's clear he can't handle the job."

"I'm a grown woman," I say through my teeth. "I don't need a babysitter."

Gabriel's jaw clenches. "A grown woman faces her responsibilities instead of running from them."

I suck in air. "I panicked. I'm sorry." My voice cracks. I expect I'll be apologizing for my rash decision for the rest of my days.

"We know," Anna says gently before pulling Gabriel aside for a heated whispered conversation. They're a good match of equally strong leaders. Villroy is lucky to have them. So am I, actually, and the last thing I want is for them to fight because of me.

I speak up. "If it's my safety you're concerned with, I have the guards and I know self-defense."

Gabriel slowly turns to stare at me. "How do you know self-defense? I thought Mother made sure you knew ballet, flute, and languages. She sent you for karate lessons too?"

"No, one of the guards taught me."

He crosses his arms, looking every bit the intimidating warrior again. "Why would he do that?"

I cross my arms too and lift my chin. "Because I asked

him to."

He turns to Anna, seeming at a loss.

"Let's take a walk before the sun sets," she suggests. "It's gorgeous here."

They leave the house and their guards go with them. I head for the kitchen for some water before heading upstairs. I want to play guitar. It might be the last chance I get before Gabriel forces me back home with an order from my king. I pluck and strum, humming along, feeling the beginnings of lift, like I almost have the feel for the song Jackson taught me. I close my eyes, letting my fingers play over the notes. The unknown wandering without a definite path is foreign to me. It doesn't sound very good. I go back to where I'm sure—my scale, the chords, back to my one song "House of the Rising Sun." Practice makes perfect. I pause at the sudden burst of conversation downstairs. Jackson and Lucas.

I quickly put the guitar back in its case, check that my hair is still in its neat chignon, and return downstairs.

"We're ba-a-ack," Lucas announces, peeling off his leather jacket. His hair and beard are neatly trimmed. "And I see you've got company, which means I can pack." He goes upstairs.

Jackson's hair and beard are also neatly trimmed, though his dirty-blond hair is still longish on top. He looks even more gorgeous than before.

"You and Lucas went for a haircut?" I ask, closing the distance between us. With Lucas upstairs and Anna, Gabriel, and the guards still outside, we're alone in the foyer. I want to run my fingers along his neatly trimmed beard, but don't dare.

"Yeah. Long overdue." His lips curve into a small smile that warms me from head to toe. He smells intoxicating, like fresh pine, leather, and sexy man. He pulls a rolled brown bag from the inside pocket of his leather jacket. "I got you sheet music." He gives me a lopsided smile, his blue eyes warm on mine.

I. Am. Melting.

Our fingers brush as I take the bag from him, a warm tingle rushing through me. "Thank you." I pull two songs from the brown bag. "Ave Maria," one of my favorite Christmas songs. The other is "Amazing Grace." Both in Italian. "I love it! Thanks so much!"

"It's nothing."

I grab him and hug him, a spontaneous impulse I've only felt with him. "It's everything." I go up on tiptoe and kiss his cheek just above where his beard begins. His cheek curves against my lips.

When I pull away, his neck is pink. Is he blushing? The legendary bad boy Jackson Walker is blushing over a kiss on the cheek?

"You're blushing," I tell him. "It's adorable."

His blue eyes sparkle. "So are you."

We smile at each other, and my heart thumps a little harder, my stomach fluttering, my nerves tingling into awareness. Oh, I remember this feeling. And for the first time I'm sure it's mutual.

The front door bursts open and Anna squeals. "Ahh! Jackson Walker! Omigod! I'm a huge fan! Ignite forever!"

Jackson ducks his head.

Gabriel scowls as Anna rushes over to Jackson. "Sorry," she says. "Omigod. It's really you. I have all your albums." She pats herself all over her body. "I need something for you to sign." She pats the top of her dress near her right breast. "Here, sign right here."

"Parlor!" Gabriel barks.

She snaps to attention, seeming to remember she's queen. I gather that's a cue word for royal protocol. "It's very nice to meet you, Jackson," she says graciously. "I'll find something later for you to sign, if it's okay with you?"

"Fine with me," Jackson mumbles, shooting me a sideways look. I'm sure he must think my family is nuts.

"Why don't we all have dinner together," Anna suggests and heads to the kitchen. "Emma, you help me prepare the meal."

I'm not sure I should leave Jackson to Gabriel. He might embarrass me by threatening Jackson for no good reason. It's not like Jackson ever laid a hand on me, though I desperately wish he would.

Gabriel gives Jackson a hard look before asking me, "Now where's Lucas? I thought they went out together."

I point upstairs and Gabriel heads that way, probably to ream Lucas for his poor babysitting job.

I look over at Jackson, feeling mushy inside. He gave me this thoughtful gift, he's been so patient with me through all my fumbling lessons, and he hasn't once been judgmental of my choice to run on my wedding day. He gets me. The new version of me, a woman who makes her own decisions and tries new things.

"Do you want to help me in the kitchen?" I ask Jackson.

He shakes his head. "I'm going to my room. Enjoy your family."

My pulse kicks harder. What if he bails because of my intrusive family? Or my family might force me back home after dinner. My stomach drops at the thought.

I can hear pots and pans banging in the kitchen. Anna is already at work.

I go to Jackson's side. "They just wanted to make sure I wasn't falling apart. Sorry for all the family intrusion. I'm sure they'll be heading back to Villroy soon." *And I still want you here with me.*

"They love you," he says gruffly. "You're lucky."

"I suppose I am." My voice chokes, and I look away, embarrassed.

He strides upstairs.

I love my family, but I can't let them keep me from him. It's one week. It's not much, but I want this time. Everything will be different when I return home. It will be like this time with Jackson never happened.

I go to the living room, staring out the window, taking a few minutes to compose myself before heading for the kitchen. I shouldn't hope for too much.

9

Emma

Anna has dinner cooking already and it smells delicious. "What're you making?" I skip the curtsy and it feels odd. She did tell me not to be so formal in private, and I'm trying very hard to loosen up my old rigid ways.

She uses some tongs to flip over chicken sizzling in a pan. "Chicken marsala here, angel hair pasta and asparagus to come. This place is fully stocked." It seems she didn't even notice my lack of formality. Perhaps my efforts appear natural.

I take a seat at the island. "I didn't know you could cook."

"Did you imagine everyone in America has a full staff to wait on them?"

"No, I just…it's a skill I didn't know you had."

"It's not hard. You can help. Wash the asparagus and chop off the thick stems."

Now that sounds manageable. I'm already handy with a knife. I make quick work of it while Anna adds mushrooms to the pan, stirring with a spatula.

She adjusts the flame and sets a timer on the microwave. "Now I'll just wait a few minutes before getting the water boiling for the other stuff." She takes a seat next to me at the island. "So you and Jackson, huh? I mean, I get the attraction, the man is sex personified, but, Emma, what're you thinking? I warned you about him. You're in all the gossip rags and the press after appearing together in Nantes. It's only added fuel to the fire. You have no idea how difficult it was for me to hold Gabriel back this long. He wants you away from Jackson and back home immediately to deal with Abdul and his family and to make some kind of statement to the press."

I'm momentarily speechless, my mind careening from gratitude to Anna for giving me what little time I've had away, to indignation on Jackson's behalf. He's not a horrible person.

"Emma, please tell me what is going on in that head of yours."

I choose my words carefully. "Thank you, Anna, for working so hard on my behalf."

"Of course. Us Rourke women need to stick together."

My eyes sting with hot tears because Anna may be the only Rourke woman who feels that way. I no longer feel close to the other Rourke women in the family, my mother or sister, and I wish it was otherwise. "Yes, I quite like that sentiment," I manage. "I just want you to know Jackson is more than his reputation. He really is, and he's been good to me. Not once has he tried to take advantage in any way and, believe me, he wants to stay out of the spotlight right now as much as I do. I trust him."

She studies me for a moment, searching my features. Finally, she says, "As long as it's just for the week. I'm a huge fan of his music, his personal character not so much."

"There's good in him." I can't help my smile. "He brought me a gift today, sheet music that I wanted for my guitar lessons."

Her eyes widen. "You're not falling for him, are you? You're in a vulnerable place right now; please don't get sucked in. You'll only get hurt. He's not going to stick around."

I lift my chin, ignoring the Jackson part to inform her,

"Actually, I don't feel vulnerable. I feel better and stronger every day."

She gives my arm a squeeze. "Good for you. Just know this, best-case scenario, you and Jackson together, which is only a slim possibility, but, let's follow it through, the family would never approve of him for you. Gabriel is a definite no, as is your mother. It would cause a lot of…tension."

"I can't always live my life according to royal dictate!" I burst out. "Sorry," I add, my cheeks burning.

A slow smile spreads across her face. "Yeah, girl! You're going through the rebellious stage you should've went through when you were sixteen. Better late than never." She points at me. "I'm going to try to get you a little breathing room." She goes back to the stove.

The tension drains from me. "Thanks for running interference. I know I've made a mess of things. I'm a mess too."

She turns to me and smiles. "You're perfect."

I shake my head. "I'm far from perfect."

"Perfectly imperfect, as we all are." She sets the spatula down and returns to my side. "So whatcha been up to?"

My jaw goes slack, shocked at her easy acceptance of my current situation. I'm so lucky to have her on my side. "Well, it's only been three days, but I've been listening to music and learning a little guitar. Jackson's been teaching me."

She looks at me expectantly, nodding, so I go on.

"And thinking a lot. Actually, today was the first time I've had time to myself in my life. I've always been surrounded by people. At home it's family, staff, and guards; at university it was other students and my guard; and out in public, there's always a crowd and guards. I blasted some music and danced like a crazy woman. I never felt I had the freedom to do that before. I know it's a small thing, but it felt wonderful."

She shakes her head. "What a sheltered life you've led. Not your fault, though, your mother kept you on a tight leash."

"You don't know my mother. You don't understand—"

She holds up a finger. "I love your mother. Since I was never adopted by a mom, I've adopted her as my own. And I know your mother didn't like me as a choice for Gabriel at first, but I'll tell you what, she brought me under her wing and very patiently taught me royal protocol and what my responsibilities as queen would be. I was well prepared, and there was not one word of malice between us. I respect her greatly and she appreciated my willingness to take on a role she wasn't comfortable doing alone. Having said all that, it's different with mothers and daughters. She molded you into her own image when she should've let you fly."

I'm quiet, thinking this over.

"Doesn't mean she doesn't love you, though. All parents make some mistakes with their kids, right?"

"I have no idea."

She gives my hand a squeeze. "They do." She glances down. "You're still wearing your engagement ring."

"It's too valuable to leave lying around. I plan on returning it to Abdul when I apologize back in Villroy, assuming he's still there."

"Oh, he's there, along with his family."

Gabriel strides in, his jaw tight. I straighten up in my seat.

Anna turns and smiles at him. "Hey, handsome. Could you set the table? The dishes are up there." She points to a cabinet across the way and goes back to cooking, assuming he will do the chore.

Gabriel goes to Anna, cups her jaw, and kisses her. "I had no idea you could cook. Is there nothing you cannot do?"

She laughs. "Well, when you set the bar that low—"

"You're magnificent," he says, and then the king of Villroy attends to the humble task of setting the dishes on the dining room table. It might be the first time in the history of Villroy it's ever been done.

It's a whole new world. One I'm not sure I belong in anymore.

~

Jackson

Emma called me to dinner, so I go, even though I feel like I'm intruding on family time. When I get to the dining room, Gabriel is at the head of the table, Anna to his right, Emma to his left. Lucas sits at the opposite end. I take a seat next to Emma, which makes Anna send a pointed look to Emma, who blushes furiously. We *are* just friends. I bet Anna has the idea that I'm about to defile the virgin princess, and maybe she's cool with it since she's a big fan of mine. Vicarious living.

Anna offers me a platter of chicken marsala.

I help myself. "Thanks."

"You must address her as Your Majesty," Gabriel snaps. "She is the queen."

I freeze. And here I thought I was polite. She doesn't seem like a queen. She's younger than me, sounds American, and is very casual.

"Oh, Gabriel, stop!" Anna exclaims. "This is private family time." She smiles at me. "Please just call me Anna."

I nod once, keeping my mouth shut. Gabriel's expression is hard, his jaw clenched tight. Emma did say he was the overprotective big brother, not Lucas, and I've already heard Lucas be overprotective. Gabriel is a thousand times worse. It won't take much to set him off.

Silence falls as platters are passed around. Emma is nearly vibrating with tension, sitting ramrod straight next to me. Only Anna seems relaxed.

Everyone starts eating, the clink of silverware loud in the silence. I'm not sure what went on down here while I was upstairs, but it couldn't have been good. After several excruciatingly long tense minutes, Anna breaks the silence.

"Jackson, Emma says you've been teaching her guitar. How lucky she is to learn from a master."

I rub the back of my neck. I've never been great with compliments. "I'm a beginner compared to some."

"No way!" she exclaims.

"I never heard her play, now that I think of it," Lucas says. "When did these lessons happen?"

"You weren't around enough to know," Gabriel snaps. "Off to Milan, off on a ride—"

"Jackson went with me on that ride," Lucas fires back. "Besides, Emma doesn't need a babysitter. Look at her. She keeps herself on a tight leash with no help from me."

"She's an innocent," Gabriel says through his teeth.

"Gabriel, I'm fine, really," Emma says softly.

I stay out of it because it's clear to me she is an innocent. She sneaks into my room and climbs into bed with me in the morning for a completely innocent reason—she's too self-conscious to let her brother see her fumble as a beginner on the guitar. It's not like she even touched…actually she did touch me, stroking my shoulder and back. I look over at her. Was that her attempt at seduction?

Her cheeks are flushed pink, her gaze on her plate as she cuts a tiny piece of asparagus. Does the virgin princess actually want me to be her first? No. Not going there. Emma brought me back the music, and I would bring her nothing but regret. But, damn, twenty-five years is a long time to wait. No wonder she seems so tightly wound, though she's been much looser during our music mornings. And when I gave her the sheet music, it was nothing, but her delighted response made me feel like a good guy for once.

"Emma would like to stay the week," Anna says to Gabriel. "I think we should give her this time away, as we originally said."

Gabriel sends me a hard look. "Will you be here?"

I lift my palms. "I can go."

"No," Emma says, shooting Gabriel a dark look before turning to me. "You don't have to go. I apologize for my overbearing brothers."

"Emma," Gabriel says gently, "you're an innocent in the ways of…" He looks at me and then stares straight ahead. "Of men like him."

Lucas snorts. "She's a virgin runaway bride. Let her have some fun. Jackson's all right."

"Lucas!" Emma exclaims.

I have no idea what to say. It seems Lucas is cool with me after our ride today.

Anna pipes up again. "If she's as innocent as you say, then she deserves this time to explore her sexuality."

Emma squeaks, her cheeks scarlet. I scratch at my newly trimmed beard. Apparently, it's a foregone conclusion that I'll debauch the princess. I know I shouldn't touch. Not just because she's an innocent or because I don't deserve her. She brought back the muse. I'd be an idiot to fuck things up and lose the music again. I can't bring myself to say any of that out loud. It would sound like I'm tempted—God help me, I am—and I'm swearing to take the high road. No one would believe it coming from me.

"Let's drop this inappropriate subject of conversation," Gabriel announces with finality. "Emma cannot—"

Anna interrupts. "Gabriel, she's two years older than me. For God's sake, stop treating her like a child. She's a stunted woman who needs to spread her wings!"

"By spreading her legs?" Gabriel barks.

Emma leaps from her seat, her eyes sparking fire. I watch with total admiration as she stands up for herself like a badass. "How dare you speak about me as if I'm not here! As if my personal life is anyone's concern but my own! I have never been so embarrassed in my life!" She gestures wildly, shooing them away. "Leave! All of you! Everyone except Jackson!"

Nobody moves. They all stare at her, eyes wide.

She tosses her napkin down, turns, and marches toward the stairs. "Jackson stays and so am I!"

All eyes turn to me.

The woman gives me no choice with that dramatic exit. I can't let her down. "Right then, I'm staying."

My gaze locks with Emma's for an intense moment, and then the doorbell chimes, breaking the spell. Her family exchange worried looks. This place is too remote for a random stranger to show up.

Viktor rushes to the door, one guard goes to the king and queen, and the other guard to Emma. Oliver must still be outside.

Viktor steps into the dining room a few minutes later and says to Gabriel, "Your Majesty, Crown Prince Abdul is here. He's left his guards in the car and is unarmed. He would like a private word with Emma."

The color drains from Emma's face.

10

Emma

My anger at my overbearing family, the brief joy of knowing Jackson wants to stay with me, all of that tangled emotion leaves me in a rush, replaced with sheer panic. My breathing accelerates, my legs tingling with the need to flee. I must calm. I must deal with Abdul. I had planned on working out a formal apology with just the right words to save face for Abdul and his family. There's no time. I glance at Jackson still seated at the dining room table. He jerks his chin at me, his eyes sympathetic.

Gabriel rises from his seat, his jaw rigid. "Did he follow us here? How did he know our destination?"

Viktor replies simply, "He greased some palms, sir."

Gabriel slams his hands on his hips. "How secure can we feel when there are people in our inner circle willing to divulge information in exchange for cash?"

"It was low-level employees at both the French and Italian airports, sir," Viktor says. "Not a staff member. This is why we have a personal security detail as well, sir."

"Is it safe for Emma to speak to him privately?" Anna asks Viktor.

Viktor nods once. "I will be in the room, Your Majesty. I

suggest you finish your dinner in the kitchen. It's the safest place in the house on the remote chance that his guards decide to leave their post in the car and take action. Oliver is with them now."

All eyes turn to me. I need to do this. Abdul deserves as much and I need to prove to my family that I can handle myself.

I take a deep breath. "Please show him in. I will speak with him in the living room."

"Ma'am, the entryway is the preferred safe location," Viktor says.

"I'm not going to force the man to stand in the entryway," I snap. "I have wronged him and the least I can do is offer him a comfortable seat."

Viktor inclines his head. "You must sit away from the windows."

"That is fine. Please show him in."

My family sends me a mixture of worried and sympathetic looks before gathering their plates and heading for the kitchen. Jackson goes with them.

I go to the living room and wait by the chair furthest from the window. A moment later, Abdul strides in with Viktor by his side. Abdul's expression is strained but not furious. His normally neatly parted dark brown hair is disheveled like he ran his fingers through it, and there's stubble on his face. I fear he's taken our parting to heart.

I close the distance between us. "Hello, Abdul, I'm glad you came. Please have a seat in the living room with me. Would you like a drink?"

"No, thank you," he bites out.

I turn and head for the chair I'd chosen earlier and indicate the adjacent sofa for him. Viktor stands next to my chair, his gaze averted. He's tuned in while giving us privacy.

"Must we have your guard?" Abdul asks. "This is a private conversation."

"I'm afraid your unexpected arrival has put my guards on alert. Please know that he is most discreet and would never reveal anything said between us unless I was in danger."

Abdul exhales sharply, glaring at Viktor.

"Which I'm sure is not the case," I add, though I'm actually not sure. I've only met Abdul on two occasions. To be fair, after I left him, he threatened a lawsuit not violence.

I take a deep calming breath and attempt to organize my thoughts, hoping above all to spare his feelings.

Abdul studies me for a moment. "I have only one question. Why did you leave me?"

The words jumble in my mind because it's hard to explain the situation at the palace, my lost place in it, my knowledge of real passion and love, which was so lacking between us, my panicked state. Finally, I say, "I am deeply sorry for my actions. I never meant to hurt you in any way. It was not about you at all. I was the problem. I wasn't ready for marriage."

His voice is low and angry. "So you run off with your lover? The rock star?"

I keep my voice calm and level. "No. Jackson is a friend. He's been staying here with me, but so is my brother Lucas and my guards. Please know Jackson has nothing to do with my actions. I was an unwanted stowaway on his houseboat docked in Villroy."

"I want to meet him."

"No," I say firmly. "This is between you and me. I'm sorry I didn't come to you with my concerns in the beginning. And after I ran away, I was in such a panicked state. I wanted a week away to clear my head."

His dark eyes turn glittering and hard. "While I have been waiting at the palace for your return. We had an agreement for marriage that left me waiting for nine years. You signed a contract."

I gulp. "I was only sixteen when I signed that. Please release me from our agreement. I know that another woman would be proud to be your wife."

He leans forward, his elbows on his knees, his voice soft.

"My family says I should've spent more time with you, a true courtship. Would that fix this?"

I choose my words carefully. "I'm sorry, no. I don't think more time together will change anything. I want love and passion in my future marriage, and I feel only friendly affection for you. I'm very sorry I waited so long to speak up."

He jerks upright. "I knew you were with that filthy man! Jackson Walker is low-class rubbish. You sullied yourself with him while pretending to be pure for me."

My lips part; I'm unsure what to say. I'm not virgin pure. I also haven't been with Jackson. "Abdul, I swear I haven't cheated on you with Jackson. He's a bystander in all this."

His eyes narrow, his voice low and menacing. "Are you pure, Emma?"

I nearly shudder. I can tell he would *not* have been happy with my nonvirgin state. I lift one shoulder, pretending not to understand. "Pure what?"

His hand is so quick I don't see it coming. The crack of a hard slap on my cheek sends my head reeling back. His lip curls. "You cheating cu—"

He's cut off by Viktor's powerful right hook that makes Abdul's head rear back. In an instant, Viktor has Abdul facedown on the floor, his knee in his back, Abdul's wrists yanked behind him. Viktor calls for backup on his wireless. Next thing I know, Abdul is in cuffs and about to be hauled away.

"Wait! Here's your ring back!" I yank off my engagement ring and throw it at him. It bounces off his forehead and onto the floor.

"Keep it!" he roars. "It's a pittance compared to the wealth of my kingdom! Villroy will have no further support from Kainei or any of our allies! Everyone will know you are the cause of Villroy's downfall!"

Then he's gone.

I drop to my chair on shaking legs and put a hand to my stinging cheek. He struck me. If I had married him, I would've been living on my own in Kainei, and he would've had power over me. His guards, staff, and family would have backed him up however he treated me. I would've had no recourse. I may even have been cut off from my family.

My gut instinct to flee was right. I'm so glad I listened to it.

~

Jackson

As soon as the guards let us, we all rush into the living room to check on Emma, everyone talking at once.

"Emma!" Anna yells.

"What happened?" Lucas demands.

"Are you okay?" I ask.

"What did he do?" Gabriel roars.

Emma stands, dropping her hand from her cheek. It's bright pink like she's been slapped. My fists clench at my sides. If only the bastard were still here to get what he deserves.

Gabriel holds Emma by the chin, inspecting the damage. "He hit you."

"It was only a slap," Emma says, sounding remarkably calm. "Viktor punched him in the jaw much harder."

Gabriel drops his hand from her and says in an eerily calm voice, "He will pay."

"No," Emma says, "let it end here. He's shown me his true colors and it's taken away all of my shame and regret for running. My gut instinct was right. And I'm sure he believes he wasted his time with me and will return home."

I slowly unclench my fists. She's all right. In fact, she sounds energized. It must be a big weight off her to be finished with the mess she left behind. Soon she'll go back to her royal life. Maybe tomorrow morning she'll pack up and go with her family. I get a hollow feeling in my chest like something was taken from me. I've only just found the music again, thanks to her.

"Viktor was a witness," Anna says. "If there is any kind of

retaliation in the press or through the courts, we have Abdul's assault to counter with."

"He cannot be allowed to get away with hurting my sister," Gabriel snaps.

Anna's lips form a flat line. "Let's respect Emma's wishes. It might be like she said that he's done with her and simply heading home."

Gabriel stalks off, and Anna follows him, speaking in a low urgent tone.

Lucas steps close to Emma. "Are you really okay?"

I hang back, but I watch her carefully because I want to know too.

She gives him a rueful smile. "Actually, I'm better than okay. Now I can truly relax, nothing hanging over me, no regrets. It's a new start for me."

Lucas kisses her forehead and walks away.

I force a casualness I'm far from feeling. I've felt protective where she's concerned the moment she showed her vulnerability back on the boat. "You shoulda punched him back. I know you've got it in you. You threw an impressive punch at my arse when I tried to throw you overboard."

She laughs. "He surprised me. Next time, eh?"

Something compels me to pull her into a hug, and I am *not* a hugger. I need to know she's okay. She feels warm and right in my arms. I lean down to her ear. "I'm glad you made it through your ordeal relatively unscathed. Not easy to do."

She looks up at me, her hazel eyes soft. "Meeting you a second time made it all worth it."

My chest constricts like she reached right in and squeezed my heart. The pull of attraction is too strong to resist. I lean down slowly, drawn in, the blood rushing through my veins. Her soft lips are only a breath away. Her eyes flutter closed, making her look even younger and sweeter. *No.* I know better than to start something with her. She'll probably be gone in the morning, back to her royal palace life, and I'm not going to be anything but a memory. Better that than a regret.

It takes all of my willpower, but I manage to step away. "Goodnight, Emma."

I turn and stride toward the stairs, needing some space between us. It's too early for bed. I'm going for my guitar before she takes the music with her. I'm halfway up the stairs when I hear her soft, "Goodnight, Jackson." It sounds wistful and full of longing.

I don't want to say goodbye yet. That hollow feeling in my chest is back, my limbs heavy as I force myself to keep walking away. *Pour it into the music and let her go.*

I'm up at the crack of dawn. The house is quiet. Why am I up? I glance toward the door, but it's still closed. No Emma. She's woken me at this time enough for my brain to expect it. Is she packing right now, getting ready to leave with her family?

I roll onto my back, tense over the coming goodbye. I should just be happy we met at all. Otherwise, I'd still be on that damn houseboat trying and failing to pick up my guitar. She gave me far more than I gave her.

She's such a good person. She forgave that arsehole for slapping her and asked for no retaliation in return. She's so good her family rushes around to preserve the goodness. She has no idea how lucky she is to have overprotective big brothers who give a shit about her. My own big brother loved nothing more than to beat me at everything. Wasn't hard to do. He was the scholar, the athlete, the good one. I was the failure. By the time I discovered music, he was already away at university. He doesn't care that I made it big. We haven't spoken in years. My mum came around, apologizing for not understanding me for so long, not realizing I had "hidden talent." We've made amends, but it doesn't change the fact that for most of my life I felt not good enough.

I roll to my other side, restless. I'm too awake now, my thoughts filled with Emma. I miss her warmth pressed up against me, miss hearing her whispering her secrets. I know she has more secrets. Why she can pick locks, for one. Maybe she secretly sneaks out of the palace on the regular and breaks into places. Maybe she's like the female Robin Hood, stealing from the rich and giving to the poor. I laugh to myself. My imagination is working overtime. She's just a sheltered princess.

Maybe one more guitar lesson before we all leave. I'll have to leave when they do, I'm only here because of Lucas's connections. I get out of bed and head for my guitar. That's when I remember Emma asked to borrow it last night after I'd finished playing. She must've been listening to me play because she appeared shortly after I returned the guitar to its case. She's probably awake. I'll just go and get it back.

I pull on an undershirt and jeans, open the door, and step into the hallway. Goose bumps break out along my arms, the hair on the back of my neck rising at the sound of her voice. She's singing "Ave Maria" in Italian and it's fucking beautiful. I creep closer, listening. Raw and real. Her emotion pours through the lyrics I don't understand but can feel. I stop outside her door, barely breathing. She hits a wrong note on the guitar, stops and strums a few times before continuing.

I slowly open the door, needing to hear her voice without the barrier between us. She's sitting on the cushioned bench seat at the end of her bed, her head tilted toward the guitar, watching her fingers as her voice hits a high note, pure and sweet, the sound reaching into my chest and squeezing the breath from my lungs.

She lifts her head and freezes, her eyes wide, her mouth a perfect O of surprise.

"Don't stop," I say. "It's beautiful."

She sets the guitar on her lap. "I missed a few notes."

I sit next to her on the bench seat. "Your voice is like an angel's. Why do you hide your talent?"

Her cheeks flush bright pink. "I didn't know I had a talent. No one ever said my voice was like an angel's before."

"Haven't you ever sung in front of other people?"

"No. I usually only sing in the shower or when I'm alone."

"Why?"

She blinks a few times and licks her luscious full lips. "I've never had lessons. I'm sure I'm a rank amateur. Everyone sounds good in the shower."

I can hardly believe she's so unaware of what she has. "No, Emma, this is special. This is amazing. Please, I need to hear more."

She bites her lip. "I don't know the song very well. I was just trying to follow along on the sheet music. Did I wake you?"

"I woke expecting an early morning guitar lesson."

She smiles. "I know you like to sleep in. I was being a pest before."

I shift closer. "You kind of grew on me."

Her fingers flutter to her neck. "Oh. Really?"

"Yeah. Go on, sing it again."

She hands me the guitar. "Here, you play it and I'll sing along."

I don't even hesitate. I take the guitar, crossing my ankle over my knee, and rest the sheet music on my leg where I can see it. I need a music stand. This is going to fall over easily. "Can you hold the sheet music?"

"I'd love to." She picks it up and stands in front of me, holding two pages up right in front of her face.

I stifle a laugh. She's shy with her singing, unaware of the beauty of it. I start playing.

She sings along softly. I keep quiet, hoping she'll get comfortable and relax her voice again. The song builds, and her voice builds with it, stronger, surer, each note achingly sweet. The music moves past the two sheets she's holding up, and I improvise, replaying chords from earlier, hoping she'll be caught up enough in the music to keep going. She does, probably because she knows this song, and it's fucking perfect. I will hear this voice in my head for the rest of my life. I've never heard the like. It's exquisite, ringing through my ears, filling my body and soul, electrifying me.

She finishes and slowly lowers the sheet music from her face. She smiles shyly, her eyes meeting mine briefly before shifting to the side. "Was that okay?"

I set the guitar down and stand. "That was more than okay. That was heaven. Exquisite perfection. You really do sound like an angel."

She smiles, shaking her head and blushing even brighter. "No."

I hold her by the chin, tipping her head up. "Yes. Take the compliment. Soak it in. You're a brilliant singer. Your voice is a gift."

She blinks a few times, her eyes shiny. "But I haven't had any lessons. I'm sure I'm not at the level—"

"Emma, you have something that can't be taught. It's a natural pure sound. The emotion. My God, I got chills." I point to my arms.

"You have goose bumps!" she exclaims. "Well, maybe you're cold."

"Emma," I growl. She's worse than I am with praise.

"Thank you for the nice compliment."

"I'm going to write some music for your voice. I'll come get you when I'm finished."

Her hand goes to her throat. "You're going to write a song for me?"

"I want to write an album for you." A rush of adrenaline shoots through me, the urgency to get started making all of my nerves light up, my muscles buzzing with the need to take action. But first—

I kiss her cheek. "Thanks for sharing your gift."

Then I go back to my room, the beginnings of a ballad rolling through my mind, the world falling away.

11

———

Emma

I sing like an angel. I had no idea. It must be true because right this very minute Jackson Walker, rock god, guitar player extraordinaire, is creating music just for my voice. I'm sitting in the hallway, leaning against his bedroom wall, listening to the beautiful sounds of a melody coming together. He's the brilliant one, composing music, creating something out of nothing.

I didn't want Jackson disturbed while he was creating, so I left my post only once to say a warm goodbye to my family. I told them I wanted to stay here for a while more with Jackson, exploring my new gift for music. Anna sent me a knowing look, Lucas bid me good luck, and Gabriel grumbled but acquiesced to his wife's insistence that I would be fine here with Jackson and my guards. The danger has passed. Our sources reported that Abdul and his guards went back to Kainei last night, and his family cleared out of the palace this morning.

The only one not on board with my extended-stay plan (or aware of it) is Jackson. He agreed to a week, but that was when I was in the midst of the biggest scandal of my life. Do I have anything that he could want that would keep him here?

I don't think even a bold seduction on my part would make him stick around long. I don't have any romantic delusions where he's concerned. He's not one for relationships, and I know my family is not on board with us as a couple anyway. Only Lucas seems to see the good in him. Anna made it clear that Jackson would only bring more scandal and the wrong kind of attention to our family. After all I've done to harm our family's reputation, I understand the need to avoid further damage.

I won't truly get involved with him, but how can I turn my back on this new musical side to myself? I've so enjoyed our guitar lessons, and now discovering my voice is something special, well, it only makes me want to delve further into the music. And I need him for that.

I'm not ready to say goodbye.

He's brought me only joy. I'm not sure what I've brought him, if anything. Maybe if I pay him for guitar lessons, make it worth his time, he'd stay on. I warm to the idea. It sounds so reasonable this way, not at all like I'm lusting after him or asking for a commitment, which I'm not. Of course I'm not. I'm merely asking for an extended visit. I'll offer my engagement ring in exchange for a month of guitar lessons at the villa. No one else wants the ring, and the diamond is worth a million euros. Even if he doesn't need the money, he could sell the diamond and donate it to a good cause, which is something I could never do under the circumstances. At least someone would benefit from it. This sounds like an excellent plan.

After my confrontation with Abdul last night, I shoved the ring in my nightstand drawer, not wanting the reminder. It occurred to me, too late, that there is no way that Abdul remained "pure" for me at twenty-six. It was a patriarchal double standard, and I almost wish I could throw that in his face, but not enough to ever see him again. I am moving on and, fittingly, he's going to help me do so by donating this ring to the cause. I slide it onto the ring finger of my left hand instead of where I used to wear it on my right.

I look down at myself and sigh. Unfortunately, my more stylish borrowed clothes are in the laundry, so I'm back in my modest pastel pink dress. I return to my post just outside Jackson's bedroom door, listening in pure rapture. He's been composing new music for hours. I've heard four songs so far. Two ballads and two rock songs with a driving beat. It's like my own personal concert. His gravelly voice sang along to one ballad, giving me chills. He didn't sing to the other songs, and I wonder if that's supposed to be my part. I so wish I could join him in there and witness the magic up close, but I don't dare interrupt his process.

The TV turns on downstairs. Viktor and Oliver must be settling in since the Abdul danger has passed. They've already checked the security system and made the rounds through the house and outside.

Jackson's door opens suddenly and he steps out. "Emma?" he calls.

I lift a hand. "Right here."

He grabs my hand and pulls me to my feet. "How long have you been sitting here?"

"Um, well, pretty much the whole time. With a brief break to say goodbye to my family."

His eyes widen. "Everyone's gone?"

"Yes."

"I didn't say goodbye."

My heart squeezes. I'm touched that he cared enough to want to say goodbye after my family treated him with suspicion, though that was mostly Gabriel. "I asked them not to interrupt your creative process. They send their goodbyes."

He tilts his head. "What're you still doing here?"

I steel my nerves. "I was so enjoying my guitar lessons with you I was hoping you'd be willing to stay on for a bit and keep teaching me. I'll pay you for your time."

"Emma," he says gently.

I cut him off before he can refuse, and hold up my hand, showing him the ring. "I'll give you this ring as payment. It's worth a million euros. Surely, you could sell the diamond and use it for a good cause. Or keep the value, if you like." I hold my breath because he actually looks like he's considering it.

He rubs the back of his neck and finally meets my eyes. "How much time?"

I take a deep breath and blurt, "Thirty days, thirty guitar lessons, and you get the ring."

He pulls me into his room and shuts the door. "Deal."

My heart races, my body humming with anticipation. I'm not sure which I'm more excited about, the possibility of a personal live concert or the possibility of him actually wanting me now. Last night he almost kissed me, and now we're alone in his bedroom. Who knows what he has in mind? I'll take thirty days of whatever he's offering. He's barefoot in jeans and a white undershirt. Super casual. We're like salt and sugar. They don't quite go together, but somehow they do. Salty and sweet. I think I'm the sweet.

I might be losing my mind to lust.

He stops in front of me, his gaze intent, his big hand coming up to tuck a lock of hair behind my ear.

I cannot breathe. My lips part, desperately hoping for a kiss.

His voice is gruff. "I like your hair down." He slides it loose from its neat chignon. Pins fly to the floor, the band around his finger. He shoves the band in his jeans pocket. "That's so much better. Looser. You hide too much of yourself in a tight package."

My mouth goes dry. "Thanks, I think."

He dips his head, his gaze direct. "Sing with me."

"Yes."

He grabs my hand and pulls me to the bench seat, where he's scribbled lyrics in a small spiral-bound notebook. His scrawl is hard to read. I see my name though, the title of a song. He wrote a song about me! It feels like a dream.

He sits next to me and smiles, a big full happy smile that lights up his handsome face. My heart flip-flops, my stomach fluttering like mad, heat rushing through me. It's the first truly happy smile I've seen on him, and he gave it to me. My hand goes to my suddenly tight chest. My eyes are hot, a lump of emotion lodges in my throat, and my lower lip trembles. It's all just so much to take in. The beauty of this moment, of Jackson creating a song just for me.

He begins to play, and I burst into tears. Happy tears, I swear. I'd be embarrassed, but I'm feeling too much joy for embarrassment to take over.

He stops playing. "What's wrong?"

"I'm just so happy, so amazed that you wrote this song for me."

He wipes my tears with his thumbs. "Look at all this emotion you keep bottled up. The smallest thing sets it off."

"It's not small at all! It's the most amazing thing that's ever happened in my life!"

He gives me a small smile. "I've heard how sheltered your life was. Now let all that emotion flow into the music. I heard some of it before when you sang 'Ave Maria,' but I think you've got more in you. Sing with me."

I hold up the notebook. "I can barely read your chicken scratch."

He laughs. "Just follow along the first time."

And then he plays it for me. *My song.* About a girl who was lost and ran, and then she stopped running and found herself. Gah. I am a mess. Tears keep leaking out of my eyes. The second verse is supposed to be mine to sing, claiming my strength, my voice, finally knowing my place. I want to be that woman, to reach that point of knowing my place.

When he finishes, he meets my eyes with a tender look. "You're something, Emma. All these tears." He cups my head, draws me close, and kisses my forehead. "Save those feelings for the music, yeah?"

I nod, trying to hide my disappointment in the chaste kiss. He's thrilled with me as a friend, as a fellow musician. Am I a musician now? Have I been sadly ignorant of my own potential all this time? It's a yes to both, I realize. I am a musician, a raw beginner, but still. The revelation makes my stomach dip like I just crested the hill of a terrifying roller coaster, and I'm in a free fall. I'm exhilarated and terrified at the same time. Princess Emma Rourke of Villroy has never stepped so far out of her comfort zone, has never risked making a fool of herself with newfound passion.

He starts playing again. "You take the second verse. Mine introduces yours."

"I know," I whisper. I still can't believe he wrote this incredible song for me. I listen, unable to tear my gaze from his beautiful expressive face. His eyes are closed, his expression relaxed, his fingers masterful on the guitar. It's extraordinary.

He opens his eyes and inclines his head for me to start my verse.

I start hesitantly, keenly aware I don't sound as natural as he does. "I lived a quiet life. I lived for you and you and you…"

He closes his eyes, playing along, seeming happy with my singing. I stare at the lyrics as I sing, building in confidence right along with the woman in the song, the music sweeping me up, my voice rising above it. I forget who I am, where I am, there's nothing but me and the music, sailing along, free.

I suddenly realize it's quiet. I slowly turn to meet his gaze, immediately self-conscious again.

"Yes," he says.

"Yes?"

He laughs. "Yes!"

I laugh too. Somehow he knows where I was at, sailing along with the music. "Is that what music is like for you too? Like you leave the world behind and you're free?"

"That's how it used to be. And just now with you singing, it felt that way again. Thanks so much, Emma."

"It's nothing, really."

"It's *everything*."

I smile and nod. "It's special. I know that. I've always loved listening to music, but now it's like I'm inside it."

He cocks his head at me. "Have you ever written lyrics?"

"Me? No. I've never written anything before."

"Ah, then this is your homework. I've got a melody in need of your lyrics."

My hand goes to my throat. "Why mine?"

"Because I want to hear your voice coming through, your soul, what speaks to you. Not as Emma the princess, as Emma the musician, the woman who rocked my world this morning."

I lean close, attempting a sexy flirtatious tone. "That sounds like we hooked up this morning."

His head jerks back. "Hooked up? The virgin princess knows of such things?" His voice is high and proper, in a poor imitation of my own.

I lift my chin. "Don't listen to my brothers. They don't know everything about me."

He sets his guitar carefully back in its case and stands in front of me, his voice low. "Are you telling me you're not a virgin princess?"

I cross my legs and rest my hands on top, pleased with the turn in the conversation. Maybe he's getting a great idea. "That is exactly what I'm telling you."

His hands form fists. "Who touched you?"

My jaw drops, shocked at his tone. "Why does it matter?"

"Because if you've been engaged since you were sixteen, it's either your arsehole fiancé or someone who took advantage, someone you trusted. And that makes me want to punch him."

"It was someone I trusted."

He sits next to me, his blue eyes hard. "Who?"

"Calm down. It was consensual. I loved him."

He shoves a hand through his hair, still looking pissed off. I'm shocked at the change in him, protective and caring. The music was my way in with him, and I wouldn't have known it if he hadn't listened to my private moment singing in my room. Maybe I need to live more out loud, put more of my true self out there publicly.

I share with him what I've never shared with anyone. "He was my guard. Adam."

His jaw clenches. "One of the guards that was here earlier with Anna and Gabriel?"

I shake my head. "He doesn't work for us anymore." I pause, memories of Adam rushing back. "When I went to university, a guard was assigned to me, a new one, very well trained. My father chose him special for me because he was skilled in martial arts and weapons. He could be lethal if needed and quiet about it."

His lips crook to the side. "So your father sent you off to university with an assassin."

I lift one shoulder. "I never thought about it like that. I suppose my father just wanted peace of mind that no harm would come to me. I was eighteen, away from home for the first time, and terribly homesick. Adam was French, but his English was quite good. He sounded like home. And he was young too, twenty-two, on his first big assignment away from home. I didn't mean for it to happen. Somehow our talks turned to longing looks and then—"

"He took advantage."

"No. I told him I loved him."

He sucks in air. "Just put it out there like that?"

"Yes." I take a deep breath, remembering the sweetness of that time. "It was all so fresh and raw, my feelings bursting out of me. I thought it had to be mutual. I couldn't be the only one feeling so much."

"Was it?"

"He didn't say as much, but then he kissed me." My fingers go to my lips, remembering my first kiss, the gentleness of it, the hesitation, the long gaze of question, the sure answer. "And I kissed him back. He pulled away, apologized, and said it would never happen again."

"But it did."

"Yes. The attraction was impossible to ignore. It became our secret." I play with a lock of my hair. "He did love me. We were together that whole school year, but when it was time to return to Villroy for the summer, he said goodbye. He quit his job and went back to France. He said he couldn't guard me properly when his heart was involved, and he knew we had no future. I was engaged to a future sultan, and he was a commoner."

"If you loved him, why didn't you break it off with your fiancé and go after him?"

I smooth a wrinkle out of my dress, considering how to answer. I don't want to sound coldhearted. Sometimes I wonder if I let Adam go too easily. I go with the hard truth. "Because I knew Adam was right. We had no future. I believed I needed to follow the path prescribed for me by long tradition, marry for the benefit of the kingdom. Adam offered no benefit to the kingdom."

"Other than love." His eyes narrow. "And here I was thinking you were so high and mighty, so much better than me. You're worse than I am. Total arsehole."

I leap to my feet and jab a finger at him. "How dare you! I shared with you from the heart!"

He slowly rises to his feet and draws close, his breath fanning over my lips, his voice a husky growl. "You deserve someone like me."

I blink, unsure what he means, my heart thundering. Is he insulting me or coming on to me?

12

—————

Emma

His hand wraps around my hair, giving a sharp tug that forces my head back and makes me gasp. His mouth covers mine, his tongue thrusting inside, and I have my answer. Lust like I've never felt before rushes through me, and I wrap my arms around his neck. He's devouring me and I love it. His hands go to the hem of my dress, and he hikes it up past my waist.

He trails open-mouthed kisses along my jaw to the sensitive spot under my ear, his teeth scraping against me, drawing a hot shiver. "I hate this old-lady dress," he whispers in my ear. "Can I take it off and toss it in the rubbish?"

I'm both mortified and immensely pleased. My wardrobe is old lady. I turn. "Do the zipper for me."

He zips it down in one quick move, pushing it off my shoulders and down my arms. I turn and the dress drops, pooling at my feet. I kick it away.

His gaze drops to my modest white bra and matching knickers. "Emma," he growls, his arms wrapping around my waist. He nuzzles into my neck, and my nerve endings light up, my breath coming harder. "So proper, so posh. I need to dirty you up."

"Yes," I breathe. I want to know what he knows, join him in the raw joy of sex. Adam was always so careful with me, so conscious of my place in the royal family and his place.

He unhooks the bra, tosses it away, and cups my breasts with both hands. "Hiding these beauties under that proper dress. It's a crime."

"I need a new wardrobe."

His eyes meet mine. "No more hiding, Emma." His hands glide down my sides, his thumbs hooking in the sides of my knickers. He pulls them down to my ankles. I am so ready for this. It's been *years*. He kneels at my feet, helps me out of them, and then his hands slide up the backs of my legs to cup my bottom. He kisses my hip reverently, softly, before shifting to press a kiss to the other hip. I slide a hand into his hair, surprised at his tenderness. I'd hoped for more aggression.

"Kiss me," I order, giving his hair a small tug, urging him to his feet.

He leans forward and kisses my sex. I jolt as his tongue darts out, flicking rapidly over me. Jesus. My knees go weak. So long, it's been so long since I've been touched like this.

He looks up at me. "Have you done this before?"

"Yes."

"Did you like it?"

Seriously? "No, I hated it."

He laughs and rises to his feet in one smooth motion. He kisses me and bites my lower lip, shocking me with the stinging pleasure. "Then I won't disturb your precious." He takes me by the hand and draws me toward the bed.

That's it? No more foreplay?

"I was joking," I protest. "Please do disturb."

He pulls the covers back, grabs me by the waist, and tosses me on the bed. I'm too shocked by the manhandling to protest. I've never been tossed about in my life.

He crawls over me, his arms straight on the mattress on either side of my shoulders. "Spread your legs and tell me what you want."

I open my legs to him and point. "I want you. Your kiss."

He slowly lowers his head and kisses me breathless. He shifts to my ear, his voice deep and coaxing. "Say the dirty words."

My cheeks burn. I can barely curse out loud and he wants me to talk dirty? "Can't you just carry on?"

He flashes a wolfish smile before lowering himself down my body. I relax because he's taking the hint, and now he'll go back to making me feel wonderful. He lingers on my breasts, his tongue flicking over my nipple, his other hand cupping my other breast. My back arches as he pinches and rolls and caresses, flooding me with sensation. His mouth closes over my breast, suckling deep, a direct line to my throbbing sex.

I moan softly. It occurs to me suddenly that the door isn't locked, and the guards will step in if I sound like I'm in distress. I can't guarantee I'll keep quiet. "Lock the door," I order.

He lifts his head. "You think the guards will come in?"

"If I sound like I need them."

"And how will that sound?" His hand trails down my stomach, making it quiver, and lower, between my legs, making me throb. "Hmm?"

I bite my lower lip, stifling a moan. "Like passion."

He grins, his blue eyes sparkling playfully. "Getting there."

He climbs out of bed, locks the door, and strips down naked. Heat pools in my belly, my womb aching. He's beautiful, all sculpted sinewy muscle, his movements sleek and predatory as he approaches, his erection thick and hard. He wants me, proper Emma Rourke. Except I don't want to be that person anymore. With Jackson I can experience the other side, the wild side.

I open my arms to him, a rare affectionate gesture, and he ignores it, instead grabbing me by the hips and shifting me sideways, pulling me toward the edge of the mattress, where he then kneels between my legs. His hands slide up my inner thighs, spreading me wider, and then finally he touches me, his fingers tracing me lightly, teasing. He blows lightly over me and my hips lift. Then his fingers trail up and down lazily, everywhere but where I need him the most.

"Jackson," I order, only it comes out half desperate.

"Yes, Emma."

"Please."

"Tell me exactly what you want in the dirtiest words you know. If you don't have them, I'll happily teach you." He flicks his finger across me and my hips jerk.

"Kiss me there," I blurt.

He gives me a naughty smile, a glint in his eye, and then surprises me, rising to his feet and getting in bed, lying on his back. "C'mere. I want you to come on my face."

I scoot to an upright position and stare at him.

He crooks his finger at me. "Come on, dirty girl. You are a dirty girl, aren't you, luv? Not a proper princess."

That is exactly what I'm trying not to be, as I shared with him when we first met. I shouldn't question his requests, I should just go along. Of the two of us, he's the expert in taking a walk on the dirty side. With fresh determination, I crawl over to him.

At the last moment, I can't bring myself to do it, so I kiss him instead. He lets me, his hand sliding into my hair, kissing me for so long I forget everything but the pleasure. He kisses amazing—deep and hot and wet, occasionally jolting me with a nip and then a soothing suck. I didn't know a kiss could hold so much. I have to get closer. I shift more fully on top of him as we kiss, straddling his erection, rocking against him, desperately craving our joining. His mouth becomes harder, more demanding, his hands roaming all over me. *Yes.* I need more. I moan deep in my throat.

He breaks the kiss suddenly, breathing hard. His hands clamp on my hips and he lifts me up his body. "Hang onto the headboard."

I grip the cushioned top, expecting him to shift behind me. Instead he shifts down the mattress, his face directly under me, staring at my exposed sex. Oh, God. "Jackson, this is…"

"Dirty? This is just the beginning. Now gimme that sweet pussy."

I close my eyes, flushed with embarrassment. I can't move. I'm caught between a lifetime of propriety and long-denied needs.

His fingers trace over me, stroking lightly. It's not nearly enough. My hips rock mindlessly, aching for him. "Come on, dirty girl. Tell me you want me to eat your pussy. That's what this is, your pussy. So wet for me, so needy."

I swallow hard. My whole life it's been referred to as my "unmentionables." It's tough to talk about something you shouldn't mention. "Jackson, please."

He slips a finger inside me, thrusting deep, and then another, his thumb stroking at the same time. White-hot pleasure spears through me. Within seconds, I'm riding his hand shamelessly, drowning in sensation. Oh God. My body clamps down on his fingers, on the edge of release, when suddenly he pulls them out. I whimper over the loss.

He holds me firmly by the hips and takes one long lick. My breath shudders out, my hips tilting toward him, eager for more.

His words run hot over my most sensitive area. "Let me hear those dirty, improper words." His finger trails lightly over me, circling my opening, teasing me.

I'm desperate for more. Closing my eyes, I whisper, "Eat my pussy." A thrill goes through me. I mentioned the unmentionable. I am *bad*.

One finger traces light teasing circles. "Did you say something? I couldn't make out the words."

"Eat my pussy," I order loud and clear before blushing furiously. What if the guards heard me? Embarrassment vanishes a moment later as he grips my hips, his tongue flicking in light teasing strokes, making me crazy. I spread my legs farther apart, opening myself to him, need drawing me in. His mouth closes over me hungrily, and I'm rocked into an oblivion of pleasure that overwhelms me, my mind shutting down.

He consumes me.

I rock against his mouth as his fingers roam, tracing me, seeming to learn me by feel. By the time his fingers thrust inside me, I'm greedy for it. My body clamps around him as he thrusts over and over, his mouth urging me on, the pressure building inside me. It's unbelievably raw, and I'm one quivering nerve, on the edge of release. Suddenly I don't want it to end. I try to hold back, focusing on anything else, the weather, my ugly dresses, wrong discordant notes.

He lifts me up, off his mouth, his fingers stroking me firmly, rapidly. My entire body trembles. "Thought I lost you, dirty girl," he rasps, his rough voice scraping against my insides. "You back now?"

"Yes," I gasp out. "Fuck, Jackson. Fuck, fuck, fuck."

And then his mouth is back, a light teasing touch that makes me quiver before he sucks hard. I cry out as the climax slams into me, my body shuddering with it. Wave after wave of pleasure floods my body as he gentles, his big hands clamped on my hips, guiding me through, letting me ride it out. Oh God. I gasp as another sunburst of pleasure rocks me, radiating all the way to my toes. Holy Jackson Walker! I have never been multi-orgasmic.

I'm euphoric. I want to hug him, laugh and dance with the pure joy of it, but I literally cannot move.

He lifts me off him and sets me on the mattress. I flop onto my back. And then he gets out of bed and walks away. I'm mildly curious where he's going, but not enough to move. I just lie there, stunned.

A few moments later, his deep voice reaches me, a hint of teasing in it. "Now, look what's become of proper Emma. Naked and spent. What's next, dirty girl?"

I crack open my eyes. He's standing next to the bed, wearing a condom, looking like a sex god I want more than my next breath. "Fuck me."

"I love hearing fuck out of that sweet mouth," he growls

as he covers me with his body, guides himself in place, and slides inside in one smooth thrust. It is glorious. A delicious ache, the joining that I craved.

He groans long and low. "So tight. Jesus. So good." He laces our fingers together and pins my hands on the mattress, rocking slowly into me, over and over and over.

The orgasm builds inside me right away, my body primed for him. "You're so good at this," I gasp out.

"God, Emma, you're something." He kisses me leisurely, tasting of me and him and sex. I can hardly believe he's being so generous. Part of me thought it would be rough, wild, and done before I even got started. His teeth close over my earlobe, giving it a tug. "You always say what you feel?"

"Only when I feel it strongly. You're extraordinary at fucking. You should get an award."

He lifts his head, his gaze heavy-lidded, a smile tugging at his lips. "Thanks."

I buck my hips under him. "Though I confess I thought it would be a little wilder."

"Too tame, eh?" He grumbles something to himself and pulls out.

I'm about to protest when he kneels between my legs, hikes my ankles over his shoulders, and presses my thighs to his chest. He grabs my hips and thrusts inside, pulling me onto him at the same time. My breath catches. He's deep and, oh God, the angle is exactly what I need, the intensity instantly ratcheting up.

I'm caught in his grip, his thrusts rough and deep and relentless. I give myself over to it, sensations rippling through me, and then everything in me coils tight. The explosion of pleasure steals my breath.

He thrusts again and again, pounding into me. "Louder. Let go. Give me everything."

"I'm d-done." It's too much, my senses on overload.

His fingers reach between my legs, stroking me as he thrusts. White hot. Intense. I'm panting, shaking, whimpering incoherently as the pleasure builds and builds and builds. The world goes dim. There's nothing but Jackson's demanding fingers, his hard thrusts pounding into me, my body coiling tighter even as he opens me up. He's talking, filthy words that wash over me in a sexy gravelly melody, driving me on. I'm nothing but throbbing pulsing need, and then I'm gone, the scream ripped from my lungs as I come apart. He holds me tight, thrusting through my release, igniting more shock waves of pleasure before he lets go with a roar, his head thrown back, the cords of his neck exposed.

My lips part at the sight of Jackson letting go, as I take everything he has to give, my breath harsh, my heart pounding. It's primal and animal and exactly what I want.

What I need.

Jackson

Now that we've crossed the line, I can't keep my hands off her. I love the way she lets go with me. I love hearing dirty words come out of that sweet mouth in her sweet voice. I fucking love that she's dropped her inhibitions, one by one, trusting me to guide her to what feels good for both of us. Her pleasure is my pleasure and that's a fucking rare thing for me. It's been four days of a hot tangle of sex and music, and I have never felt so creative, so alive. Shagging is different with Emma. I want to see her eyes, her expression, the wide-eyed shock, the heated desire, the soft look of dazed bliss. I'm hooked on the high of getting Emma off.

I'm in bed, it's early morning, but I'm up because she's up, moving around the room. No matter how late I keep her up, she wakes at dawn. It's Saturday and we're heading into Milan later so she can get some clothes "that suit her new lifestyle." She kills me with her proper words. I've taught her all the dirty words I know. She cracked me up, sharing every euphemism in the book for dirty talk, including proper medical terms. Now she loves using dirty words, her face lighting up with pride at claiming them. Yeah, I did that.

I snag her wrist as she walks by my side of the bed. She jumps. We're in the master bedroom now and I have a side. It would freak me out more if I didn't know this was just a holiday. Thirty days of guitar lessons, one huge-arse diamond ring to complete the transaction. Only it's not that mercenary. I would've stayed longer without payment, but the value of that diamond means I can set up a trust for Charlie's son, Jack, that will give him a real chance out there. That kid didn't ask to be born into such a shitty situation.

Besides, the time limit makes living with a woman manageable. I'm not committed. I can just enjoy her.

She leans down and kisses me. "Did I wake you again? I tried to be so quiet."

I grab her, pulling her over me. "You're turning me into a morning person."

"Really?" she chirps. "Let's get ready and go shopping, then. I'm going to pick out some jeans that fit and some outrageously impractical high heels."

I roll her onto her back and undo the tie on her silk robe, spreading it open. She's all luscious curves and smooth pale skin. I nuzzle into her neck, breathing her in. She smells amazing, fresh from the shower, her shampoo like vanilla and honey. I can't help but touch and taste, peeling off her robe and kissing every exposed delicious inch of skin.

"I thought you'd be spent," she says. "I sucked you off just an hour ago. Your cock can take more?"

I groan, feeling myself get harder. The sweet dirty talk is the biggest turn-on. "This is why I'm a morning person now." I nuzzle into her breasts, cupping them, grazing my thumbs across her nipples, feeling them tighten to hard buds. I suck one nipple into my mouth, drawing deep, and her back arches, offering more. She's shockingly open, her reactions honest, her expressions unguarded. It only makes me feel more protective of her.

I kiss and lick and nip my way down her body.

She sighs, her fingers sliding through my hair, her legs opening for me, inviting me in. I slide a hand down to find her hot and wet and ready. Normally that would be my signal to move full steam ahead; instead it just makes me want to make her wetter. I lever my body down, pull her legs over my shoulders, and dive in. She tastes like honey and sex. It's fucking crazy how good she tastes.

Her hands lose their grip on my hair, her hips arching up, begging for more. And I give it to her. I need it as much as she does, need to hear her break. Her soft cries, her harsh breaths, her "fuck, fuck, fuck." It's a beautiful thing. I tease her a bit, shifting my mouth away, playing with my fingers, thrusting inside her, adding more fingers, making her moan. Fuck. Now I need to be inside her. She's tight velvet heat, like heaven.

"Fuck me," she demands.

I groan. It's like she knew I needed it too. "I will. First I need to hear you break."

"You want me to scream? What? I'll do anything if you just fuck me."

I'm pulsing with need. "Hang on." I climb over her to grab a condom from the nightstand and she strokes me. "Baby, stop. I'm not going to last."

She gives me a sultry sexy smile and licks her lips, leaning toward my throbbing cock. Jesus. I taught her too well. I shift away, roll the condom on, and nudge her onto her back.

She opens her arms to me, and I shift into her embrace, her arms and legs wrapping around me in an intimate hug. My heartbeat roars in my ears, and I'm suddenly finding it hard to get a breath. Her eyes, shades of green and gray with a golden ring, are warm on mine. Loving. I've never felt love. Not like this.

She gives me a soft smile, reaches down, and guides me inside her.

I surge forward, sliding a hand under her hip, lifting her to meet my thrusts. The heat, the rush of oblivion, clears my head. I can breathe again. Nothing but tight heat, honey and vanilla, soft curves, driving need. Over and over and over.

Mindless fucking.

Eyes closed.

The only sound our bodies slapping together.

I shift near her ear. "Say my name when you come." I need it. I don't know why.

She grabs my head, our eyes lock, and then she trembles under me. "Jackson," she says softly, lovingly.

I close my eyes, fighting the pull of that softness. I drive into her urgently, desperately, and then I hear her break, the soft cry of my name falling from her lips, giving me what I asked for, giving me everything, and I let go, the rush overwhelming me. I hold her tight against me.

I'm not sure how I'm going to let her go.

13

Emma

Life is good. I have never felt so happy in my life. I've never had so many orgasms in my life either. Jackson surprised me with his generosity in the bedroom. And the music we create fills my soul. I'm in love with the whole world today.

We're about to go to Milan, but I need to check in with the guards first. I find them in the kitchen, sipping espressos. "Good morning."

They snap to attention. "Good morning, Your Highness," Viktor says.

"Good morning, Your Highness," Oliver echoes.

I had a talk with them the morning after Jackson and I hooked up, informing them that we were now a couple and I would appreciate them keeping that to themselves since we weren't ready to go public with it yet. This was not exactly the truth, the couple part, but I want our privacy. Jackson may well leave after the thirty days we agreed to; he may even object to the idea of us actually being a couple. I don't know what he's thinking. All I know is he's not Mr. Commitment.

And I'm halfway in love with him.

I know it's crazy. It's too fast. And I swore to myself to keep it casual, knowing his reputation, knowing my family wouldn't approve. Maybe what I'm feeling is just all the crazy good endorphins from the orgasms. I *was* long overdue. I flush at the memory of this morning's orgasm and concentrate on getting myself a cup of espresso. I could use the caffeine. Jackson is a night owl and keeps me up late. He's figured out that, even if I go to bed at my regular time, all he has to do is softly strum his guitar nearby. It's like a siren song, a seductive irresistible pull on my body and soul. Next thing you know, the guitar is back in its case and I'm straddling his lap. Of course I'm still up at dawn. Damn internal alarm clock won't ever snooze.

I take a sip of espresso and turn to the guards. "We're going shopping in Milan today. We'll be taking a motorcycle." I'm planning on riding behind Jackson.

"Ma'am, I wouldn't advise that," Viktor says. "For your safety, we'll take you in the car." He means the rented Mercedes with tinted windows. I'm forever riding in them.

"Jackson is an experienced rider. I'll be safe with him. You may take the second bike if you'd like or meet us there in the car."

Viktor frowns. "We'll get back to you on the arrangements, ma'am."

I head for the living room and take in the view of trees and rolling hills. It's a little chilly to go out to the lake, so I shift over to the family room with its large window to admire the lake view from here. I haven't heard from my family and I take that as a good sign. They're giving me some space, something I never really needed or asked for before. I suppose once Jackson leaves, I'll go home. It'll be close to Christmas, and I've never missed a Christmas with my family. If I'd gone through with my marriage, I might never have had another Christmas back home. I wonder what Jackson does for Christmas. I push that thought away. I'm not going to invite him to spend it with me. Even if he has some feeling for me, if I just blurt out my feelings like I did with

Adam, it could backfire and scare him off. Better to just enjoy what we have now and play it by ear.

I smile to myself. I'm learning to do that more now, playing it by ear. I practice guitar diligently, but I'm also letting my fingers play to see where it might lead. You know, that is a good way to live, letting myself play and seeing what happens. It's much better than rigid rules and routines. And, so far, this new way of life has only brought good things, beautiful music and a wonderful time with Jackson.

A short while later, I head up to the master bedroom to see if Jackson's ready yet. He's dressed in a gray thermal shirt, black jeans, and black motorcycle boots, his hair a little damp from the shower. His gaze collides with mine, and I'm suddenly breathless. One look from those heated blue eyes is all it takes.

He stalks toward me, wrapping an arm around my waist and walking me backward until my back hits the wall. His head slowly lowers, his eyes smoldering, his lips curving into a slow sure smile. "I like you in these jeans."

I stare at his mouth, stupid with lust. "My laundry returned today. I thought they would be better for the motorcycle ride than my dress."

He slides a hand under my hair, cupping the back of my neck with a warm firm grip before his mouth crashes over mine, rough and demanding. I wrap my arms around his neck and return the kiss passionately. A moan escapes as he lifts my leg, grinding into me. Sparks of pleasure shoot through my core, radiating outward. I'm already wet, my body primed for all he makes me feel.

He pulls away suddenly and runs both hands through his hair, grumbling something to himself. Then he grabs his leather jacket from the back of a chair and pulls it on. "Let's go."

I follow him out to the hallway. "What's wrong?"

He stops and half-growls, "What's wrong is you're too damn tempting all the fucking time."

I hide my delight, fighting back a smile. "Maybe it's you that's too damn tempting all the fucking time."

He brushes his thumb over my lower lip before pushing it into my mouth. I suck his finger, my gaze on his heated eyes. "Fuck," he growls and pulls me back into the room, kicking the door shut and locking it.

We slam together in a furious frenzy, ripping our clothes off as we kiss and bite and suck. In a flash, he turns me, bending me forward and pushing my palms flat against the wall. His heat sears my back. The first thrust makes us both groan, and then it's fast and hard and deep, a primal race toward the finish line. He's urging me on, his gravelly voice in my ear, a torrent of filthy words that thrill me. His hand slips between my legs, his fingers driving me closer and closer to the edge. My vision dims, and I break violently, harsh cries ripped from my throat as I shudder under him. He's right there with me, thrusting deep, his breath harsh in my ear. "Luv," he says and lets go, pumping into me in hot spurts.

My head drops. Slowly, reality returns and, with it, two disturbing truths. That wasn't love, it was just a luv.

And we forgot the condom.

~

Jackson

I forgot the fucking condom. Idiot. See, this is the power she has over me. I have never forgotten the condom, not even when I was flying high or pissed on too much whiskey. Always the condom. It's Emma. She's too much.

I rub the back of my neck. "Hey, don't worry, I got a clean bill of health six months ago." I finally got a physical after I dropped all my vices. I got the all clear and told myself I'd stay that way.

She lifts a shaky hand and smooths her hair. "I'm good too, so you don't worry either." She lets out a little laugh. "I'd better go wash up." She grabs her clothes and rushes to the loo.

I want to bail. It's a shite move, but things just got serious as fuck. I yank my clothes back on. What am I even doing here with a princess? Then I remember our deal. The diamond ring that could set up Jack for life. That's a decent reason to stay around, even though I feel dirty, in a bad way, for the exchange of sex and money. It was supposed to be for guitar lessons. Bloody hell, I botched this deal beyond repair. That's what happens when I lead with my dick.

Truth is, money aside, the bigger problem with Emma is it's *not* just sex. I can deal with walking away from great sex. I've had it before, I'll have it again. Though her combination of sweet and dirty is new for me, an irresistible combination. Okay, it is the sex, but it's also the music. It's back for the first time in months, rumbling through my mind, and what we create together is better than anything I could do on my own. She's starting to come up with melodies and counter-melodies. She hums or sings the notes and I pick it up on the guitar. I've been thinking of adding piano too, something I haven't wanted with Charlie always being the one on the keyboard. I've been thinking of getting her into the studio, recording her voice.

I've been thinking too much is the problem.

She returns a few minutes later, dressed and composed. She gives me a small smile. "Well. That was another new experience. I'm really living it up now, aren't I? Taking a walk on the Jackson side."

My back gets up for no other reason than I'm entangled with her and I don't even know how I got here. "Is that what I am? A diversion for you? See how the other half lives?"

She presses her luscious lips into a flat line. "I didn't say that."

"You should. I am after all just a commoner, an unedu-cated, self-taught rocker. That doesn't exactly fit the royal prince you're meant for."

Her eyes flash. "I was engaged to a prince and left him.

What's your problem? You're the one who forgot the condom."

I cross my arms. "You're the one who went along with it eagerly. Don't tell me you didn't feel the difference skin on skin."

"I was too far gone!"

I throw my hands up. "So was I!"

She shakes her head. "Jackson, this is crazy. What're we fighting about? We forgot the condom. It happens. Let's go."

"That's it? It happens, and let's go shopping?"

She nods once. "Yes."

"What if you're pregnant?"

She looks up to the ceiling and back to me. "It's too soon to know. It's probably fine."

"A child out of wedlock to a rocker? That's going to go down well with your royal family."

"I can't worry about the what-ifs." She takes a step toward the door, and I snag her by the arm before she can make her escape.

"Humor me. What if?"

She stares at my chest. "He or she would have royal blood, which means my family would likely take me in, and the child will want for nothing."

My gut clenches. Obviously I'm not needed for any part of this picture. I should be glad, but I'm pissed off. It's like she said "thanks and so long!" It's not like even *once* in my life I imagined myself married with a family. I don't know any happy families, no solid marriages. Relationships always crash and burn, which is why I avoid them. I should get out before I get in any deeper. She doesn't need me. Maybe I don't need her either.

But am I really going to abandon a child like my arsehole father? Abandon Jack's chance at a secure future? He's four years old. Fuck.

"I'm sure we have nothing to worry about," she says firmly.

She's in denial, which is probably how she ended up

bailing at the very last minute on her wedding. Denial all the way up to the end. Only this time it's with me, and I'm not letting it go that easily. "When will you know?" I ask.

She chews her bottom lip. "I don't know. Things were a blur of wedding planning and activities. I lost track of my cycle."

"So we just play it by ear?"

She smiles. "Yes, we do. And you know what? Playing it by ear has been working really well for me."

I shake my head. This is not at all like improvising music. "We're getting you a pregnancy test. You can take it in two weeks, yeah? Or three? Let's get a few. We have to be sure."

"I'll have Viktor get some on a clandestine mission. He can be trusted to be discreet."

"A clandestine…yeah, okay." I fucked things up big time. The worst, most idiotic part is I *want* to go shopping with her. I want to see her dress like a normal twenty-five-year-old instead of an old lady. I want to see her letting go and enjoying life. It's almost like I'm discovering life right along with her. I'm hooked on Emma. She's the drug I can't quit.

This can only end badly.

"Jackson?"

I take a deep breath and refocus on her. "Yeah."

"Did you, um, want children?"

"I never wanted to be a family man."

"Oh. Okay. Shall we go?"

Something isn't sitting right. She's too easygoing about this whole baby business.

I take her hand and tug her against me, wrapping my arms loosely around her waist. She looks up at me. "Ready for round two with condom?"

I hold her jaw, my thumb sliding across her soft cheek. "Listen. I…I don't know anything about being a father. My own dad split when I was two. I don't even remember him. I'm not sure I'm cut out for this."

"Now you listen. We'll play it by ear. Everything will work out." She hugs me, her cheek pressed to my chest. I can't help but wrap my arms around her. "Jackson, I'm in love with you."

I stiffen and drop my arms from her. "No."

She looks up at me, her arms still wrapped around my middle. "You don't have to feel the same way."

I scowl. "You should *want* someone who feels the same way. Don't accept less. This is why you ended up running away from your wedding. You just accepted a loveless marriage."

She jerks away. "Don't judge me when I'm speaking from the heart! I will rip your hair out by the roots, jab you in the throat, and-and kick you in the balls!"

My God. She is perfect. I think I love her too.

I can't help myself. I yank her against me and kiss her. I can't seem to stop.

Fuck me.

14

———

What-ifs scare me. I was prepared to produce an heir for Abdul after our marriage, probably right away. I was not prepared for whatever this is with Jackson.

I refuse to spend the rest of my limited time with Jackson worrying about something that might not even happen. So I'm completely focused on the now. I'm on the back of a motorcycle for the first time in my life, my arms around the man I love, the Italian countryside breezing by. I'm wearing his leather jacket because the moment we stepped out to a chilly November day, he took his jacket off and put it on me. He cares about me. I don't need the words to know. The jacket smells like him, and I never want to take it off. Does it bother me that he didn't say he loves me back? Not at all. He kissed me passionately after I said I love him. Adam was the same way at first. I think sometimes men can't say the words, so they show it instead. I feel it in his touch, in his gaze, in his gloriously happy smiles when we create music together. That is more than enough for me.

Viktor is on a second motorcycle in front of us. Oliver took the car for our purchases and is behind us. I don't anticipate any problems shopping in Milan at this time of year since it's not tourist season. And Viktor is more than capable of dealing with any unwanted attention on the two of us.

When we arrive, we park the motorcycle on the street and head to the main shopping district with its fashionable boutiques. Here I am shopping with three men in tow. Ha! You'd never catch my brothers shopping. Viktor stands guard by the door. Oliver takes a seat near the dressing area.

The saleswoman, a brunette in her fifties with oversized glasses, welcomes us, and I greet her cordially in Italian. I can feel Jackson's stare, and I give him a smile. He's astounded I know so many languages, but it's like music in a way. I have an ear for it, always have. I spoke English and French equally well when I first spoke at two years old (my nanny was French), and my mother was so delighted with my skill, she brought in native speakers to chat with me in Italian and Spanish as well. The romance languages—French, Italian, and Spanish—have a lot of commonalities, so it's not terribly difficult, and I had ample opportunities to visit those countries when I was older to practice the language.

I browse the racks with the saleswoman's assistance. Soon, a dressing room is filled with a variety of modern dresses, skirts, jeans, and trousers. Tops follow, ranging from silky blouses in bold patterns and bright colors to cute T-shirts with cap sleeves. I've never enjoyed picking out clothes so much in my life. This is for the new Emma, the one who lives out loud.

I go into the dressing room and start trying things on. The first dress is a long-sleeved black jersey material, much too tight in the waist.

There's a knock at the door.

"*Si?*" I ask, figuring it's the saleswoman.

Jackson's voice rumbles through the door. "Let me see your outfits."

I open the door.

He nods appreciatively. "Not bad."

I run a hand over my stomach. "It shows my gut too much."

His hand slides over my stomach. "No, luv, you've got curves. Get that one."

I smile uncertainly, looking down at myself. My dresses have always been chosen to hide my curves as much as possible.

He holds my chin, his gaze direct. "Trust me."

I do. I probably trust him too much, but so far he's been good to me. "Okay. Next outfit." I shut the door and peel off the dress.

He whispers through the door, "After this, let's get you some sexy lingerie."

I smile. "Do I need to try it on for you?"

"Nope. I'll pick it out. You just wear it."

"What if I don't think it suits?"

"Well, who's going to be the one drooling over it, eh? Me or you?"

I laugh. "Right."

I let out a happy sigh. I've never felt so desired, so sexy. Jackson can't keep his hands off me. I don't need a label for what this is when I feel this wonderful. Surely, there's nothing to worry about.

Two weeks later, I'm floating in a sea of love, music, and sex. I have never had so much deep satisfaction in my body, heart, and soul. I wake at dawn, as usual, and slide my hand over a sleeping Jackson. He's on his stomach, which gives me ample opportunity to trace the flames of his tattoo over his shoulder blades. He grumbles in his sleep. Maybe my touch was too light. I smooth a palm over him, sliding across his wide shoulders and down his back. He's naked. We both are from last night.

He likes me to stay in bed with him in the morning, but since I can't sleep past dawn, I typically lie here cuddling him and listening to music in my mind. I hear the songs he's taught me, the songs I practice to, and the new songs he's written. He has a new one about growing up a misfit angry at the world, fighting his way through. I love the emotion he puts into it. The chorus concludes we're all misfits. I love that too. I have never been angry at the world, more like numb to it, but I have felt like a misfit with all the changes at home since my father died. I'm learning to be okay with not being the perfect princess anymore. I'm defying expectations. Me. Defiant. It really is a whole new Emma.

"We should get you some ink," he says in a sleepy voice.

My hand stills on his back. I cannot add body art or piercings, except for ear piercings, as a royal. It's considered desecration of my body, and I would not be buried in the family plot because of it.

"What should I get?" I ask because I am a rebel.

He props up on an elbow, leans over and kisses me. "My name."

"Where?" I whisper, the idea thrilling me. He wants to keep me, to let everyone know I'm his.

He rolls me to my stomach and slides a hand to my lower back just above my bottom. "Right here. Jackson."

I smile. "Too bad I can't desecrate my body, because I would love that."

His hand slides over my bottom. "Desecrate?"

"I'd be kicked out of the royal burial plot for altering my body, except for earrings. Those are acceptable."

He groans. "Sometimes I can almost forget who you are."

I'm proud of that. I'm dressing to please myself, exploring music for the first time, and enjoying the hell out of my first lover since I was eighteen.

He gives my bottom a light pat. "Today's the day. Go take the test." He means the pregnancy test. A few days after our slipup, I left denial land and wondered what if? Would Jackson stick around for a child? I know I would keep it. I've always wanted children. I went through the calendar on my phone, trying to jog my memory, and realized that today would mark one week late, which is a good time to test. I'm almost positive I'm late due to stress.

What if?

Okay, it wasn't all sunshine and roses these last two weeks. There were moments, scary moments, where I imagined no Jackson in my life and a constant reminder of him through our child. In any case, today's test should show definitive results.

He gives me a nudge. "Get up."

I stall. "Right now?"

"Yeah. First thing in the morning."

I don't move. It's not that I'm afraid of a pregnancy. I would welcome a child once I got over the shock. I'm just afraid it will be the end of me and Jackson. We have eleven more days together, but he might be so spooked, he takes off, ring or no ring.

"Why're you not moving?" he asks.

I fake a yawn. "I'm tired."

Next thing I know, he's got me over his shoulder, one hand on my bottom, walking us toward the bathroom.

I give his bottom a pat. "I like when you go caveman on me. No one has ever manhandled me the way you do."

"That's because I pretend you're a regular person, not an untouchable royal. That's going to bite me in the arse."

I bite his arse for that.

"Ow!" He swats my arse in retaliation, and I laugh.

He sets me down in the bathroom, grabs the pregnancy test hidden under the cabinet, and hands it to me. "Pee on this."

My jaw drops. "Pee on this? Could you be more crass?"

"Yeah. Pee on this stick while I watch, and tell me if you're up the duff."

I take the test from him. "Get out."

"Five minutes." He leaves.

I shut the door and lock it.

His voice carries through the door. "Hurry up. I need to know."

Geez, no pressure. I don't know if I can pee with him standing on the other side of the door listening. "Go away!"

"Are you pee-shy, babe?"

I've never heard the term, but it seems that I am. "Yes. And I need a sweater. A jumper," I amend for his British speak. "It's chilly in here."

A few moments later, he knocks on the door. I open it and he shoves my sweater at me. "Run the water. I'm going to play guitar."

"Thank you."

I pull on the soft sweater, run the water in the sink, take a small paper cup, and help myself to several drinks to make this go easier. I can hear him playing. He's not singing along, probably because he's listening to me. So I sing. It's the song he taught me at my first lesson, "House of the Rising Sun."

I finish singing and get quiet. I want to hear him.

He starts playing one of his new songs. I listen and think about what our child would be like, raised with music. Two musical parents would likely produce musical children. A lovely musical family. What if?

I lean against the sink and listen to more songs. It's easy to get lost in the music when Jackson plays. Finally, I get down to business, reading the directions and then taking the test.

I set it on the back of the toilet and count, my eyes never leaving the stick. Yes or no, stay or go? I don't know if Jackson will stay if it's positive. He was very ambivalent about it. He said he never wanted to be a family man. I don't need him to be, but deep down I would like him to be. I would like to have a future with him. Who knew that three weeks ago stumbling across his houseboat would lead me to this moment?

Time's up. Negative.

I'm both relieved and let down. Silly. I'm young. There's plenty of time for children in the future.

I open the door, and he's right there. I hold up the stick. "Not pregnant."

His whole body relaxes. "Right. Great."

I toss it in the rubbish bin and wash my hands. "I guess that's that."

He spears a hand through his hair. "I'm so relieved. Aren't you?"

"Yes, of course."

"We should celebrate."

"Sure, maybe later. I'm going to finish getting dressed."

"You want to play my guitar?"

I brush past him. "I think I'm going to take a walk. Clear my head."

"Oh-kay."

I stop and turn back to him. "Would you have stuck around if it was positive?"

"But it wasn't positive."

"So no."

His face distorts into an expression that says it all—repulsion at the idea. "I don't know."

"Ah."

He holds up his palms. "It's a lot, Emma. And you have to admit, your life would be very different tied to mine."

I can feel myself shutting down, my defenses going back up, the walls of proper Emma protecting me. "Yes, well, I suppose it's a moot point."

I finish getting dressed and then, head held high, take my jacket and go for a walk, my guards trailing behind me.

Jackson

Emma is upset. It's been two days of silence on the Emma front. I don't know if it's because she's disappointed not to be pregnant or because she's disappointed in me. All I know is that she stopped singing, stopped playing guitar, even stopped humming. She told me that she always has a song in her head, but I think it went quiet in there. It *kills* me. I know what it's like to lose the music, and I fear she's lost what she only just discovered.

I've been playing more guitar, trying to coax her back, but all she wants to do is read and take long walks alone, though the guards follow her everywhere. I can see how easy it would be for her to fall for a guard; they're her constant companions, more than anyone else. She's been going to bed early, getting up early, not interested in sex. She even stopped cozying up to me in the early morning. I'm losing her. Any moment she'll hop on the jet and fly home, never to be seen again.

On Monday I do the only thing I can think of, I go for a motorcycle ride in search of a gift. I do care about her, even if I don't want to be tied down.

I return in the afternoon to find her watching another Italian soap opera on the telly. "Hey, Emma, I'm back."

She doesn't turn from the screen. "Hello." Her tone is flat.

I grab the gift I left in the hall and return, holding it out to her. "I got you something. A surprise."

She looks up and does a double take. I hand her the case with a big red bow on it. It's the first week of December and they had gift wrapping at the shop.

She slowly stands and closes the distance, her eyes glued to it. I hand it to her and she sets it on the floor, carefully opening the case to reveal a Gibson acoustic guitar in a light rosewood. It's a thing of beauty I would've loved to have when I was starting out.

She stares at it for long moments. I think I shocked her with the gift. Finally she reaches out with one finger, lightly stroking the glossy wood.

"Give it a try," I urge.

She gingerly carries it with her to the sofa and strums a few notes.

I follow her. "It's a Songwriter Deluxe made for musicians who compose their own songs. The tonal quality is excellent."

Her hazel eyes are huge. "I can't believe you gave me this. I'm overwhelmed. You really see me as a songwriter?"

I sit next to her. "Absolutely. You hear the music in your

head. You know the basics and can employ someone to help with composing the more advanced stuff."

She stares at her guitar, caressing the fret and the wood body. "It's the most beautiful present I've ever received." Her voice is breathy, reverent, and my chest fills with pride. I did the right thing with this gift. She lifts her head. "Thank you, Jackson, so much. You've given me more than I can ever repay."

My throat chokes with emotion because I should be the one saying those words. I can barely speak over the lump in my throat. "You've given me far more. I was empty, lost, in total despair that I'd lost the music. And you brought it back with your sweet voice, your talent, your eager willingness to learn. It made me remember what it was like to first open up to the music. You've given me more than I ever thought possible."

Tears leak out of her eyes, and I brush them away, kissing her soft cheeks, her nose, her lips. I close my eyes and speak against her lips the words I never thought I'd say to anyone. "I love you."

"I love you too!"

We stare at each other.

I don't know where to go from here. She puts the guitar back in its case.

Then she climbs onto my lap, straddling me, wraps her arms around my neck, and kisses me passionately. She's back. I'm so relieved all of me relaxes. Lust, music, love all mixed up together in one royal package. I don't know what I'm doing with her, why she loves me, but I'm tired of questioning it.

I hold her soft curves tight against me, my hands roaming, needing to feel her all over again. Two days of no Emma love was torture.

She breaks the kiss and eases off me, shifting to stand in front of me. "Let's go upstairs. Privacy."

I realize with a start the guards must be nearby. I'd forgotten about them. They're such a quiet presence.

I join her upstairs, and the moment I close the door and lock it, she throws herself at me in total abandon. God, I missed this. Her eager enthusiasm, her openness. I'm a starving man, and she is a feast.

She runs for a condom and hands it to me. Like it's her responsibility now.

I take it from her, and she immediately strips naked. Need surges through me. Still, I want her to know the pregnancy scare wasn't her fault. "Emma, it was on me before. I should've remembered the condom."

Her fingers nimbly undo my jeans. "As long as one of us remembers. Hurry. I've missed you."

I strip down and roll it on in record time, the urgency in her voice driving me. I'm not gentle. I can't be. I pin her against the wall, lift her, and take her in one hard thrust. Her nails dig into my shoulders; her legs wrap around me, her eyes hot on mine.

Deep and hard. I take and take and take.

I'm in deep.

So deep. I can't stop.

I angle her back, slipping a hand between us, stroking her rapidly. Her body clenches around me, and I lose control, my release roaring through me, dimly aware of her soft cries as she pulses around me. We collide and explode. Every fucking time. I collapse against her.

She grabs my head and kisses me, her eyes bright, her smile huge. "My family wants me home for Christmas. Come with me."

My first reaction is to say Christmas is past the thirty days we agreed to. I'm supposed to be leaving with her ring in a little over a week. Then I feel like a total arsehole because I said the big I love you, which implies a relationship. My gut rolls, my heart thumping hard, belatedly agitated over being tied to another person. Somehow I fell head over arse into a relationship without knowing it. The time has just been flying by in a haze of music and sex. And then I thought I'd lost her and it was bloody torture, and then I got her back. I'd be a fool to turn her down. "Yeah, okay."

Her eyes widen. "Yes?"

"Yes."

She laughs and kisses me all over my face. I hold her tight, spent and well loved. Only I can't escape the feeling that the palace is the last place someone like me belongs.

15

Emma

Jackson and I are on the royal yacht heading for the port of Villroy on Christmas Eve. We've lived together for almost six weeks, an unusual way to begin a relationship, skipping all the dating and courtship part. I'm sure other people would say we're an unusual pairing, but it works. We have music in common, and I suppose I always had a thing for an edgy man. After all, my first love was a guard as skilled as an assassin. Jackson brawled when he was younger, but the Jackson I know has mellowed. He's a deep soul.

The pregnancy scare is behind us, especially once I got right back on track with my cycle the day after he gave me my very own guitar. I suppose my happiness with him broke through all that stress and got my body on track.

Jackson has been a little jumpy during our travels today back to my home. I'm nervous too. I checked in at home about Jackson joining us for Christmas after I invited him. Anna was fine with it, but when I followed up a couple of days later asking how the rest of the family was taking it, she said, "I'm the queen and I say it's okay. Don't worry about it."

I worry.

I don't want a rift between me and my family. I love them, and I love him.

I take a seat in the small dining area of the main cabin, where Jackson is nursing a beer before sunset. "Are you okay?"

He stares out the window. "Yeah."

I search my mind for something to reassure him about spending time with my family and come up empty. I don't know if it will go well, so it seems wrong to assure him it will. I tell myself to focus on the positive. Jackson is willing to spend Christmas with me and my family because he loves me.

He looks at me with hooded eyes. "I never did get that ring you promised."

My stomach drops. I'd thought the exchange was unnecessary. That was incentive to make him want to stay with me. I jump up, adrenaline racing through me at what this could mean. "I'll get it right now."

I head up to the captain's perch, where Viktor is standing with the crew.

He crosses to me immediately. "What's wrong?"

My cheeks flush with shame. Jackson is using me. He'll likely go straight to his houseboat when we arrive at the port in Villroy with my diamond ring in his pocket. "I'd like my ring back, please." I asked him to hold it because I didn't want to wear it upon returning to Villroy, but feared it might too easily get misplaced in my suitcase after the staff took care of unpacking it.

Viktor doesn't question it. He merely gives me a curt nod and says he'll retrieve it from the yacht's safe. Even for this short journey, he's been careful with it, knowing its value.

"Thank you," I manage. "I'll wait here." I don't want him to see me handing it over to Jackson.

I cross my arms, hugging myself, chilled by the air, even colder on the inside. All my happy warmth has deserted me. A few minutes later, Viktor returns and palms my hand, handing it to me.

"Thank you." I slip the ring back on my finger, flashing back to when I first received it at sixteen, the first time I met Abdul. How adult I'd felt, how stupidly starry-eyed. Now it's a mercenary trade for a few lousy guitar lessons. Except it was so much more than that to me. My eyes sting, my throat tight, crap. I can't cry in front of everybody. I ruthlessly push all that unwelcome emotion down.

I return to the cabin, where Jackson is gazing out the window. His familiar blond hair, casually mussed as usual, the wide slope of his shoulders, his scruffy bearded jaw. All of it permanently etched in my mind, seared on my heart. Suddenly I'm furious. How could he have led me on like this? Why didn't he leave with the ring when the thirty days was up? That was last week. Not one word about our deal back then. What the hell is he doing going home with me for Christmas?

I stop next to him, yank off the ring, and toss it at him. "Here."

He straightens and the ring clatters to the floor. He reaches down to scoop it up, and I barely resist smacking the back of his head. "Thanks."

I clench my teeth, biting back a sarcastic reply.

He stands and shoves the ring in his jeans pocket. Completely casual. Like none of this matters. Like *I* don't matter.

"Is that all you have to say?" I demand. "Thanks?"

His brows draw together. "I appreciate it."

I seethe. I feel like a complete fool, the way I opened my heart to a heartless man. "Well, goodbye."

One corner of his mouth lifts. "Going swimming?"

"No. I'm just going to another area of the yacht. Giving you some space." I hold out my hand. "We'll say goodbye here."

He stares at my hand. "Did I miss something? I thought I was going home with you for Christmas."

I swallow hard. Was I drawing the wrong conclusion?

Maybe he really needs money *and* he wants to be with me. I'm afraid to ask. My heart feels like it's twisting inside out.

I drop my hand and speak to his chest. "I don't know. Maybe you want to go home for Christmas."

He pinches my chin, tipping my face up to his. "Did I say I wanted to go home for Christmas?"

I blink rapidly, fighting for composure. "No."

His fingers shift, cupping my jaw. "What did you work yourself up about? You nervous about going home?"

It wasn't that, but, yes, I am nervous. I don't want to make things worse, my feelings are all tangled up, so I simply say, "I'm fine."

His eyes narrow. "Define fine."

"Perfectly okay."

"Is it the ring? You want to keep it for the memories?"

"No!"

"Right then, I give up, babe. You're about to cry for no reason that I can think of."

I let out a shaky breath. I cannot explain without exposing my fear that my deep feelings for him aren't returned. Maybe his "I love you" was only to lead me to this point of handing over the ring. My gut knots. This is the dark underbelly of love, that clawing fear after so much happiness that the love can be taken away. It's like that diamond between us, shimmering with beauty yet sharp enough to cut glass.

He pulls me into his arms, and I melt against him, my entire body flooded with relief. His strong arms, his solid chest, his warmth, his sexy scent. This is right. Why do I doubt?

Jackson

I slide a hand under her hair, cupping the back of her neck as she presses her cheek against my chest. I tried to play it cool, but inside I'm in a cold panic. Emma must've sensed I was having second thoughts. Meeting her family? Her mother? This is serious. I've never committed to any woman. Never wanted to. And they're going to take one look at me and know I don't belong. Emma is one of the elite. And though I might have some status as a rock star, I've never felt elite. I'm scrappy street and she's posh palace.

I seriously considered locating my houseboat, which is supposed to be docked in Villroy, and heading home. Not to spend Christmas with my family either. The last thing I want is to visit with my mum and watch her fawn all over my perfect brother and his perfect family. I planned to do my usual, go on a bender and perform at some seedy pub. Charlie used to go with me, which is why it doesn't appeal. John and Max, my other bandmates, actually like their families.

She draws back and tips her face up to me. Her eyes are clear now, no more threat of tears, her expression relaxed. I actually feel calmer too. It's strange how powerful a simple hug can be. I can't resist kissing her, a soft press to her luscious lips.

She smiles. "My mother will die when she sees this dress." It's a clingy red halter dress with a deep V cut in front that shows off her lush cleavage, and ends modestly past the knees. It's so Emma—sexy and sweet. I fucking love it.

I slide a finger along her exposed collarbone and dip into her cleavage. Her nipples harden into points, and she shivers. I love how she responds to my touch. I nuzzle into her neck, breathing in the soft scent of vanilla and honey, trailing up to her ear. "Scandalous."

Her voice is breathy. "It is. Shoulders and cleavage must be covered, you know."

I wrap her hair around my fist, loving that she wears it down now. "Will you get in trouble for not following the royal rules?"

She runs her fingers through the hair at the nape of my neck. "It's the royal protocol. I won't be punished, if that's what you're asking. The new queen, Anna, well, you've met her, she's much more relaxed about protocol. My mother will be disappointed in me, but she's already disappointed. She took me running from my wedding as a personal betrayal and wouldn't listen to my apologies. I can't live my life to please her anymore."

I still, an alarming thought making me go cold. "Am I part of your rebellion?"

She smiles mischievously. "I suppose when I first met you, I thought you'd be perfect for a rebellious act, but I don't see you like that anymore. You're like me, in love with music, deeply soulful, and passionate."

I can't help my smile. That is me. And her. "Brilliant. Do you still feel lost?"

"You helped me find my true self."

Everything in me relaxes. If I just focus on Emma, on the here and now, the agitated gotta-escape feeling eases. I want to be better than that. For her.

I point out the window as Villroy comes into view. "There it is."

"Home," she says reverently.

The island is striking with rocky cliffs, sandy dunes along the beaches, and dotted with white cottages with blue doors, shutters, and window frames all along the winding road leading up to the palace. The palace is stunning on top of the hill, an imposing sandstone structure with multiple towers and spires. It's fairy-tale beautiful.

"Hard to believe you live there," I say. "It looks like something from olden times."

She beams, staring at her home. "This version of the palace took shape after a fire a couple of centuries ago. I've always loved it. Don't worry, it's been modernized. My people have called this island home since way back when the Vikings first settled here, bringing their Irish wives from an early Irish settlement. I've always felt such a deep sense of belonging, of taking my place in a long tradition."

That ugly voice in my head pipes up. *This is where Emma belongs. Not you.*

"I broke that tradition," she says quietly. "I've changed."

Her voice rises in panic. "What if I don't belong here in this new version of me?"

I give her hand a squeeze. "You're like this palace, yeah? Same Emma just modernized."

She laughs. "I love that. You have a way with words. No wonder you're a great lyricist."

Heat prickles my neck. I'm about to say there's better out there, when she wags her finger at me. "Accept the compliment."

That's what I tell her when she tries to downplay her musical abilities. She's got something rare and special. I grab her wagging finger. "Thanks."

A short while later, the yacht docks at the port, the crew rushing around to secure it. Bloody hell, the paps are here, reporters too with microphones and cameras. I should've known. I didn't have to do any digging at all to see the bad press online about Emma dumping Abdul and his mouthing off about her cheating on him with me. Lies, but who cares about the truth when it's a juicy story? I'm sure me showing up with her now will only add fuel to the fire. Emma went from a crown prince and future sultan to an inked rocker with a nightmare of a public-relations problem. Imagine if she was up the duff on top of everything else. They'd have a fucking free-for-all with an out-of-wedlock pregnancy. She'd never live it down, and there'd be no doubt in anyone's mind that I'm bad news.

I squeeze her hand. "We have an audience."

She glances over at the waiting crowd of piranhas and grimaces. "I expected as much. Preparations had to be made for my arrival, so word got out. Just ignore them. I've been lucky to avoid the press for as long as I have." She peers out the window. "There's your boat waiting for you if you want an escape." She knows I'm supposed to lie low.

"I'm not leaving you to the mob."

She presses herself against my side, wrapping an arm around my waist. "Hard to believe just six weeks ago, I was puking on that thing."

I grin. "Yeah, too much tequila."

"Probably that and the Cocoa Puffs."

I suddenly remember how furious I was over the Cocoa Puffs and how I haven't had anything like it in weeks and haven't cared. Just shows how narrow my world was back then, wallowing in the misery of losing Charlie and the music, hanging on to a stupid box of Cocoa Puffs.

Viktor opens the cabin door. "Ready when you are, Your Highness."

Emma turns to me and says brightly, "Ready?"

I incline my head and pull my leather jacket on. I have a really bad feeling about my part in all this press for Emma.

A few minutes later, we're walking across the dock toward the road, where three Mercedes are waiting. Emma's sexy red dress is covered by her long white wool coat. She stands out in white among a sea of black coats. She grabs my hand in a death grip, her chin up, shoulders back as rapid-fire questions are shouted at her.

"Emma, Emma, over here! How long have you been with Jackson?"

"Have you heard the sultan cut ties with Villroy and is advising other kingdoms to do the same?"

"Any comment on the limp sausages in office, Jackson?"

"Is he better in bed than the sultan?"

"Are you still a virgin?"

A ripple of laughter goes through the crowd. I want to punch that guy with the virgin remark, tell them all to go fuck themselves, but I know from experience that will only make it worse. I have to settle for glaring at the wanker who dared speak to my Emma that way.

Emma lifts a hand and smiles. "It's great to be home, everyone. Merry Christmas! *Joyeux Noël!*"

A few reporters mumble, "Merry Christmas" and "*Joyeux Noël,*" and then the questions start again. She's addressed them politely in English and French. You ask me? She's given them more than they deserve. Hell, she's given me more than I deserve just by being herself.

Viktor hustles us to the middle car, taking the front seat. Oliver gets into the car behind us. The car in front must have more guards.

"Welcome home, Your Highness," the driver says.

"Thank you, Arthur," Emma says pleasantly. "I've brought my boyfriend, Jackson, home for the holidays."

He eyes me in the rearview mirror. "Very well. Welcome to Villroy, sir."

"Thanks." I turn to Emma. She has a fake smile plastered over her face, her hands folded together in a grip so tight they're white. I pry one of her hands free and hold it. I lean close, keeping my voice low just for her ears. "Ignore the bloody reporters. They don't know you, and they have no right to know you."

She stares at our joined hands and says under her breath, "I am a public figure. I serve Villroy and must make myself available to them." Her voice is stiff and proper, her back ramrod straight. Shades of the posh and proper princess I met on my houseboat are showing through. I should've expected it. Soon she'll go back to her old ways. I won't fit in her life anymore. I was a diversion in a time of distress.

I'm pissed off, though I have no right to be. I take a deep breath. "That doesn't mean they can disrespect you."

"I didn't answer any disrespectful questions, did I?"

I turn and look out the window at the cottages as we wind up the hill. I imagine these little cottages were for the peasants back in the day, where my people would've lived. The elite always live at the top of the hill.

16

Jackson

The car pulls up to a front courtyard, and the moment we step out, several men wearing white shirts with black trousers approach, welcoming Emma home with great deference, bowing to her before escorting us to the double palace doors. She doesn't introduce me to the servants, just greets them and keeps walking swiftly toward the entrance.

Another servant opens the doors for us, and I get my first look at the inside of a palace. The two-story white marble entrance hall with gilded mirrors and silk wallpaper looks like something out of a museum. Only a large Christmas tree with white lights and white ornaments in the corner warms the cavernous space. No wonder Emma was so uptight growing up in a museum like this.

More servants line both sides of the hall. I have no idea what they each do, but they're waiting with smiles for Princess Emma. No one seems put off by her running away from her wedding. They're just happy their beloved princess is home. Emma is gracious, polite, extremely proper. Like a completely different person from the one I've got to know these past weeks, letting loose with her voice and her body. Here she's all contained.

Emma squeezes my arm. "This is my boyfriend, Jackson, everyone, here for the holidays."

The servants murmur greetings to me. I lift a hand. "Nice to meet you all."

A man steps forward to ask Emma a question in a low voice I can't make out. She smiles brightly. "Yes. Please bring everything to my suite. Jackson will be staying with me."

I relax a little. She's openly acknowledging my place in her bedroom, which is very improper.

She turns to me, smiling, and winks. "I wouldn't want you to get lost trying to find my room in the middle of the night."

I slide a hand to her neck, giving her a stroke down the side with my thumb. This is the Emma I know.

By the time we're in her suite of rooms, after passing through a maze of hallways decorated with oil paintings and marble busts of a horde of royal ancestors, I'm feeling out of sorts again. The scale of everything—the sheer size of the palace, the long proud tradition—all of it is foreign to me.

Her maid, Lina, bustles around the suite, which is like a flat with a living room, sitting room, whatever that is, large bedroom, and en suite bathroom. The suite is very feminine, mostly pink and floral with carved antique wooden furniture full of curlicues and carved legs. The walls are pink floral, the lamps have matching shades, as do the curtains framing large windows with views of the sea. The canopy bed is virgin white from the gauzy sheer fabric over it to the white blankets. There are far too many pink pillows. This is a room a man has never breached.

Yet here I am.

I take a seat on a pink and white floral chair in her bedroom, attempting to blend. What I really want to do is grab my guitar, which is in the sitting room next to her guitar, play it and drown the world out. I can't be too grumpy though. I'm a guest here. Besides, Emma brought music back to me, so I can deal with a delay in playing my guitar. I shift uncomfortably, the ring in my pocket digging into my thigh.

Better find a hiding spot for it. I head to the sitting room and stash it in my guitar case's compartment inside a small pouch that holds picks. It's safe there until I can get back home and exchange it for cold hard cash. I can't sell it through an auction house without exposing Emma. It's too recognizable. I'll have to track down a trustworthy jeweler and offer just the diamond separate from the setting. It's a weight off my mind to know Jack will be taken care of.

I return to the bedroom chair and watch Emma in her "scandalous" red dress as she directs Lina, who's unpacking Emma's things and placing them in drawers and in the wardrobe. My Christmas present for Emma is a song. She doesn't need any material things, and it's the one gift I can give her that no one else can. Well, they could, but it wouldn't be a Jackson Walker original.

Lina turns to me. "Would you like me to assist you with your things, sir?" She indicates my oversized duffel bag.

"No, thanks." I'm not unpacking. I don't belong here. It's a temporary gig before I move on. It occurs to me that Emma will want to stay here. After Christmas, we're finished. I drum my fingers on my leg. We could meet up, I guess, but right now seeing Emma in her element, I just can't see where we fit.

"Will there be anything else, ma'am?" Lina asks Emma.

"We're good. Thank you, Lina," Emma replies formally, the height of princess manners.

It sets my teeth on edge, this bizarrely overly polite Emma with servants who address her so deferentially.

Lina bows her head and leaves, quietly shutting the door behind her.

"Your Highness," I drawl.

Emma crosses to me, a determined expression on her face. Before I can say *alright?* she surprises me, hiking her dress up to her waist and straddling me in the oversized chair. I'm instantly hard, my hands sliding up her smooth bare legs, cupping her bare arse. She's wearing a thong, part of her new wardrobe. She leans down and bites my lower lip. My cock surges against my jeans. "You, Mr. Walker, owe me a hard fuck."

I slide a hand to the scrap of fabric between her legs, and she moans. "Do I now?"

"Yes." She sticks her plump lower lip out in a pout. I'm fixated on those porn-star lips. "You were so busy watching me pack this morning and playing guitar, you completely neglected me."

My voice comes out hoarse. "Maybe you were so busy packing this morning, it was you who neglected me."

She kisses me roughly before sliding to her knees in front of me, reaching for my zipper.

I groan. I've got my Emma back.

I'm on my way to an evening service at the palace chapel, feeling completely out of place again. First, I'm not a chapel kind of guy. I haven't been to church since I was a kid. And, second, I didn't pack anything nice enough for a royal Christmas Eve service. I don't know why I didn't think to pick up a suit in Italy, and Emma didn't mention it, but now I'm wishing I had something better than a long-sleeved gray cotton shirt, black trousers, and black motorcycle boots. Emma changed into a dress from her old wardrobe, a modest long-sleeved pale green sack that ends way past her knees. You can barely tell she has a waist let alone fantastic tits in this getup. Her hair is pulled back into a bun. I'm getting whiplash watching her morph from sexy vixen to proper princess. I'm not sure which one is the real Emma anymore. Is she just putting on a show for me and being herself with everyone else? I can't help but think I'm a novelty for her, a plaything to try out stuff she normally can't do. My gut churns at the thought.

I follow her out the door of her suite, and she loops her arm in mine as she leads us through another maze of hallways. I'm not sure I could get out of here without a map.

We're nowhere near where we came in. A staircase comes into view. At the bottom are more servants lining the way, for what purpose I have no idea. Greenery wraps around the ornate wooden banister. There's another large Christmas tree in the downstairs hall, which is not the main hall. This tree is decorated all in blue and silver with numerous balls, icicles, and snowflakes.

"Look what the rock star dragged in," a familiar masculine voice drawls, "my errant sister. Tsk-tsk, Emma. What would Mother say?"

It's Lucas, grinning up at us. Her brother is always taking the piss out of her. He's dressed in a navy blue suit, somehow seeming more relaxed in it than Emma in her formal clothes.

"You tsk-tsk," Emma returns with good humor. She told me she used to get very worked up over her older brothers' teasing, but plans to be more relaxed about it.

"Lucas, good to see you, man." I shake his hand, and he pulls me in for a bro hug.

"So it must be serious if you're here for the family Christmas," Lucas says. "I'm surprised—" He catches Emma's glare and turns back to me. "I mean, glad to have you here." He leans in and lowers his voice. "Didn't think Emma was your type."

"I heard that, Lucas," Emma snaps. "Mind your business."

Lucas mimics her, mouthing the words *mind your business*. Emma ignores him and walks ahead of us.

"Emma's cool," I tell him. "She can sing like an angel. We've been making music together."

Lucas elbows me in the ribs. "Is that what the kids call it these days?"

Emma stops and turns a murderous glare on her brother. "Don't you have somewhere else to be?"

He scratches his beard, giving me a sideways look. "It's Christmas Eve service. You don't want me to be a sinner, do you?"

Emma lifts her chin and grabs my hand, walking quickly,

working hard to outpace her brother. He keeps up with us. I'm starting to understand why Emma bonded with her mum if she had four older brothers harassing her like Lucas. She has a younger brother, too, but she says Adrian isn't much of a teasing type.

Lucas is firing questions at her, questioning her angel status since I said she sings like an angel. My bad. "Is your halo gold or silver? Who's polishing it? Are your wings primly taped under your matronly dress?"

It's clear he loves her, even though he gives her a hard time.

Emma shuts him up with one question. "How's Mother?"

Lucas gets serious. "Not good. Still holed up in her room."

"Is she coming to service?"

"I don't know. Anna and Gabriel begged her to join us, but she didn't say one way or the other."

Emma entwines her fingers with mine and whispers, "It's our first Christmas without Father."

"Ah. Sorry."

She nods solemnly and turns to Lucas. "If she's not there, I will visit with her after. I know she's very unhappy with my behavior, and we should clear the air."

"Good luck," Lucas says.

A few minutes later, we arrive at the chapel, where two men in suits wait, who must be Emma's brothers. Like Gabriel, they have short dark brown hair, angular cheekbones, and clean-shaven square jaws. Lucas is the only one with a beard.

Emma beams. "You two cleaned up nice. No scruff."

They both rub their jaws like it's something new. "Temporary for Christmas," one of them mutters.

Emma makes the introductions. "Jackson, these are my brothers Oscar and Adrian. Adrian's my younger brother who has a twin, Silvia, whom I told you about."

"Big fan," Oscar says, shaking my hand.

"Never heard of you," Adrian quips.

I laugh. "That's fair."

Adrian grins. "No, seriously, I'm a big fan too. Very cool to have you as our guest."

"Where's Phillip?" Emma asks. That's her brother too. She gave me the rundown earlier.

"He's spending Christmas in Tampa with his fiancée's family," Adrian says.

"Traitor," Lucas says.

"To the dungeon," Oscar says.

Lucas and Oscar grin at each other.

Adrian gestures to the chapel door. "I guess we should go in. We were waiting to meet you." He looks right at me.

Emma waves that away. "I know I've gained some notoriety as a runaway bride, but you needn't fanboy over me."

I laugh, and her brothers stare at her.

"Emma, is that you?" Oscar asks, peering closely at her. "Did you actually make a joke?"

"I told you she cracked," Lucas says. "No more proper Emma, though Jackson says she has the voice of an angel, so maybe there's some extremely good girl lingering in her."

Adrian smiles. "Emma used to sing when we were little. I always liked it, but she stopped singing when we got older."

Emma tilts her head. "You know, I'd nearly forgotten I used to sing out loud. I suppose I stopped around nine years old when I first started etiquette lessons and understood my place in royal life." She smiles brightly. "And now I'm back to it." She opens the chapel door and steps inside.

I follow her in, my eyes widening at the imposing space. It's worse than the grand entrance hall in terms of royal greatness. It's one of those soaring ceiling, gilding on every-thing, hand-painted, carved stucco kind of places that make you feel insignificant. Along the sides are alcoves with multiple marble apostle figures and hand-painted royal markings. At least they have music. Maybe too much music. Three enormous gilded organs with long silver pipes. I bet a commoner never set foot in here before.

"Oh, everyone's here, even Mother," Emma whispers to

me. "That's a very good sign." She points out her mum sitting on the end of the front row. Anna, sitting next to her mum, turns and waves to us.

Gabriel glances over and inclines his head. Some other older people are in the row as well. Relatives? I have no idea.

Emma leads me to the second row, stopping to greet her mum. "Mother, it's so good to see you at service. This is my boyfriend, Jackson."

I offer my hand, and her mum stares at it like it's a smelly dead fish.

Her gaze rakes over my casual outfit and she sniffs. "I'm glad to see you're home, Emma. I would like to speak to you after service." She faces front, dismissing us.

Emma's expression is tight as she shifts further into the second row. Her brothers join us, Adrian taking a seat next to me. He leans over me to whisper to Emma, "You're in for it."

"Shut it," she whispers back.

We sit there for a long time in the quiet of the chapel as more people arrive. "Are these the servants coming in now?" I whisper to her.

She shakes her head and whispers, "These are relatives on my mother's side. They've travelled a distance to support her in her grief. She's from a small island kingdom near Australia. Not that she asked for their support. I suspect Anna had a hand in this. She's forever forgetting royal protocol. We keep our emotions and personal needs quiet. Always the kingdom and our people above ourselves."

"What about your father's side?"

"We don't talk about that."

Adrian quietly fills me in. "My father's older brother abdicated the throne to marry a commoner. He was exiled. His family has no connection to ours, except through our sister Silvia. Now that she's living in the US, she looked them up."

Lucas leans over. "The Rourke riffraff."

They chuckle, and Emma glares at them, hissing, "Keep the dirty laundry out of sight."

Her mum glances over her shoulder at Lucas, purses her lips, and faces front.

Emma jabs a finger at her brothers and inclines her head toward their mum.

I whisper in her ear, "Since Anna is a commoner, will she invite the riffraff side back?"

Emma shakes her head. "Unlikely they would ever be accepted. Anna had to really prove herself, and she didn't come with a bad reputation."

Now who does that remind me of? Bad rep, commoner, riffraff. I try not to fidget on the hard wooden pew. "Where are the servants?"

"It's a family service," Emma replies. "No servants."

"They're not allowed?"

"They have their own chapel in the servants' quarters. It's a nice room."

"A room?" *Compared to this?*

"Yes, a quiet space for them. Or they can go to church on the island. There are a few."

I look around at her family, all dressed in custom-made suits and formal dresses, the expensive jewels glinting in necklaces, bracelets, rings, and earrings, their regal bearing. Under normal circumstances, I know exactly where I'd be, with the servants. The two of us alone in Italy, I let myself forget who she really is. The differences between us have never felt so stark.

I can't fathom why she brought me here. Soon enough she'll realize her mistake.

17

—————

Emma

I'll admit it was a bit surreal to return to the palace chapel after going through my wedding rehearsal only six weeks ago, but it felt very different with the Christmas greenery and holiday candles, and I felt very different on the inside, though I did my best to blend on the outside. I do want to make amends with Mother.

"I'll meet up with you in a bit," I tell Jackson once we're in the hallway after service. "I'm going to talk to my mother. Go with my brothers to the private salon for cocktail hour. I'll meet you there." I go up on tiptoe to kiss his cheek, mindful of our audience.

He cups my jaw, his thumb brushing my cheek. "My night sounds better than yours."

"I'm sure it will be fine," I say, keeping a stiff upper lip.

He joins my brothers, who're waiting nearby, talking to some of our relatives. Everyone has gathered in the hall, chatting cheerfully in a festive holiday spirit. I don't see my mother. I assume she headed back to her room.

I go straight there, determined to bridge the distance between us. I'm going to explain my actions on my wedding day and the subsequent transformation, no, *discovery* of myself as both a musician and a woman. I'll tell her how happy I am and how much I'd like her to be part of my life again. I will not mention her rude dismissal of Jackson. Mostly because my future with him is uncertain. His boat is nearby, he has the diamond ring, and, honestly, I don't know where we go from here. It isn't something I wish to discuss with Mother, however. Whether or not she meets me halfway or shuts me out, I have nothing to lose given how things are between us.

I make it to her room, pumped up and ready to say my piece. I knock and her longtime maid, Joan, answers, opening the door wide. "She's in the sitting room, Your Highness."

"Thank you, Joan."

I'm glad my mother hasn't retreated to her bed yet. Maybe she's ready to return to us. I find her sitting at the table by the window. She loves the view of the sea. Though it's dark now, she still stares at it.

"Hello, Mother." I lean down and kiss her cheek. Her skin is alarmingly thin and papery, not soft like it used to be. She's lost more weight too while I was away.

I take the seat across from her. "Have you been eating?"

"Of course." She lifts a hand. "Please give us some privacy."

Joan bows her head. "Yes, ma'am." She leaves the suite.

My mother stares at me for an uncomfortably long time. Her hazel eyes match mine, though hers look bleak. "You look well," she finally says. "The time away has been good for you."

"It's been wonderful. I've been staying at Lucas's friend's house on Lake Como."

"I'm aware."

I gulp. "Mother, I'm finally happy. I needed to step away from palace life to discover myself. I can sing. Jackson says I have real talent. We—"

"I cannot believe you brought such an inappropriate guest to our family holiday," she says, her eyes flashing. "I want him gone. He's been a terrible influence on you. This on top of your previous behavior embarrassing our family, why, I feel like I don't even know you anymore."

"I'm still me. A less rigid *happier* me."

She scowls. "I want my daughter back."

I lose it. "And I want my mother back! You do nothing but hide in your room. It's like I lost you and Father on the same day."

Her lips press into a flat line. "So this is the cause of your rebellion. Me. Always blame the mother." She leans forward. "I have done *everything* for you, given you every advantage, poured time and energy into shaping you into the woman you needed to be. Now you turn against me."

The words come tumbling out. "You shaped me into a mold of yourself. But guess what? I'm not you. I'm finding out who I am. I like to dress in bold colors now, not pastels. I'm done hiding behind clothes, behind protocol. I like to sing; I *love* to sing. I'm learning guitar. I have talents I didn't even know I had because I wasn't open to anything. All the rigid rules and expectations stifled me. Now I'm free, and I'm sorry if you don't like this Emma, but this is who I am from now on."

Her lip curls. "This is *his* influence. This man who doesn't dress for service, who shows no respect to our family."

I clench my jaw, ignoring the jab at Jackson. "This is me. Nobody else."

She looks down her nose at me. "I know his type. Low class. Drugs, alcohol, women. You're nothing but one of many in a long line of more to come."

"That's not true! Jackson isn't like that."

She shoos me away. "Then go live with him in his hovel."

I try again, reaching for patience. "You don't know him. He's been good to me, and I'm sure he lives in a nice place."

"Leave. He's turned you into a person I no longer recognize." She turns back to the window, dismissing me.

It's like talking to a wall! I'm so furious I'm shaking with it. "I spoke to Abdul in Italy and gave him my humble apology, and what I got in return was a hard slap in the face and verbal abuse. This is the man you wanted me to marry."

She turns to me, her voice softer now. "I heard about that. Emma, there was nothing in his background to indicate—"

"Obviously you don't always know what's best for me." I shove my chair back so fast it nearly topples over. I right it and take my leave.

I stalk down the hallway. For God's sake, I'm a grown woman who finally knows what she wants. Why can't she see that I'm capable of changing on my own? I'm not so weak-willed as to be shaped by someone else's influence. Yes, I've embraced Jackson's music lessons and his taste in lingerie, but that doesn't mean I'm not making my own choices. The music we create together reflects both of us. The rest is still me just a new empowered me. That's the problem here. Mother can't handle an empowered Emma. Well, too bad. I'm never going back to the old proper me, bowing to duty and obligation.

I go to my room and change out of my hideous dress, part of the old Emma wardrobe, and pull back on my red halter dress. I love it. It makes me feel sexy and more like a woman than a girl dressed for a part. I take out my chignon and brush my hair out. Then I refresh my makeup, liberal with the smoky eyeliner and red lipstick that matches my dress.

By the time I finish, I've gone from furious to sad. I don't know how to fix things with Mother, and I'm truly worried about her. She hasn't been the same since my father's passing. I shake off the melancholy and head down to the private salon in search of Jackson. I need to grab that feeling I had in Italy with him. That empowered, brilliant kickass energy that made me feel alive.

I find him sitting on a leather sofa, my brothers gathered around him and on the sofa across from him. He's a novelty to them, a rock star. To me, he's my love, my gateway to passion and music and life. My eyes well unexpectedly, my throat nearly closed with all I feel for him.

His eyes collide with mine and he stands, crossing to me, standing close but not touching. I need his touch.

I hug him, wrapping my arms tightly around his waist. He bands one arm around my waist, his other hand sliding under my hair and cupping the back of my neck.

His voice is a rumble near my ear. "I take it that didn't go so well."

I lift my head, keeping my voice low. "She thinks I'm awful and that you're a bad influence on me. She told me to go live in your hovel with you. She doesn't understand."

He drops his hold on me and gives me a sympathetic look. I check on my brothers. They're ignoring us, laughing and joking around as usual.

"It's okay," I assure him. "I explained what's going on with me and with us too. There's nothing more I can do."

"Emma…"

"What?"

He shoves his hands in his pockets. "I don't want you to be on the outs with your family because of me."

"It's not you. It's me. I've dared to step out of the box I was put in. So, fuck it. Right? Life moves on."

"I suppose so," he mumbles.

"I would like a drink," I say brightly and head to the wet bar.

Jackson stays behind. I can feel his gaze on me. I'm determined not to let my fallout with my mother dampen the evening.

A short while later, we all head to the dining room for a family Christmas Eve dinner. It's quite full with Mother's relatives here, some of whom I haven't seen in years. Everyone is here except Mother.

Anna looks distressed over my mother's empty chair, and after a brief conversation with Gabriel, she leaves. I look to Gabriel in question.

"She's going to get Mother," he says, reading my expression correctly. I've always felt in tune with my oldest brother with our shared sensibilities in doing our duty to the crown.

He's loosened up quite a bit since meeting Anna. Maybe that's what Jackson is to me, the male Anna. I smile to myself at the thought.

I glance at Jackson and give his thigh a squeeze under the table. He doesn't respond. Normally, he'd give my hand a squeeze or put his hand on my thigh, indecently slipping his fingers wherever he pleased. Lucas says something to him and he turns away.

I take a long swallow of wine, mentally preparing myself for the possibility of my mother showing up. Will she be rude to Jackson? Will she ignore me like I'm no longer her daughter? Acid burns in my stomach.

I take some bread, though it isn't proper to eat before everyone is seated, and quickly follow up with the remainder of my wine, draining my glass. A servant immediately refreshes it. What am I worried about? Anna won't be able to get Mother to make an appearance. I don't care what Anna says about adopting my mother as her own, the reverse is definitely not true. My mother has been tolerant with Anna and her outspoken brash ways, but she doesn't treat Anna like a true daughter. They haven't spent time together beyond the bare minimum required for the transfer of the queen's duties from Mother to Anna.

The room erupts in greetings as Anna returns with my mother in tow. My jaw drops and I quickly snap it shut. How did Anna get her here? Especially after the nasty fight I just had with Mother. I thought she'd stay holed up in her room for another year. Maybe she didn't care enough about me to be distressed. She's washed her hands of me. Nausea rises in my throat.

Everyone stands, bowing their head to the former queen. She doesn't smile, merely lifts a hand in acknowledgment of everyone, and allows Anna to escort her to a seat near the head of the table where Anna and Gabriel sit.

"Now that we're all here, I have an announcement," Anna says.

The room gets quiet.

She beams. "I'm pregnant!"

Everyone choruses congratulations. Lucas whistles and my mother sends him a withering glare. Not proper behavior.

My emotions are all over the place, my eyes welling with tears. So much is happening at once. Of course, I'm happy for them. Also, a little jealous. I would love to have an adoring husband and child on the way. I hazard a glance at Jackson. He looks uncomfortable, staring at his plate. I tell myself it's because he's not used to my family, not that he's anti-family. But that's not exactly true. He said it himself—he never wanted to be a family man. I shouldn't fantasize about what will never be.

Gabriel is smiling from ear to ear; his gaze for Anna is pure adoration. "She's eight weeks along. Due early August. We couldn't be happier."

"Or more nauseous," Anna chimes in. "I've got two weeks of morning sickness so far with more to come. Alexandra, you'll have to tell me how you managed with six pregnancies." That's my mother.

My mother actually smiles. "I was lucky. Never had morning sickness." They have a quiet conversation, my mother looking livelier than I've seen her in forever. I wonder if this is how Anna got Mother down to dinner, by telling her she'd be a grandmother. My mother has been adamant about the necessity of Gabriel producing an heir. He's done his duty, but anyone can see he's thrilled to do so.

Gabriel signals for dinner, and soon we're all enjoying the first course, sautéed scallops with foie-gras sauce and fresh truffles. Villroy being a major seafood supplier, caviar, smoked salmon, and lobster soon follow with various side dishes and palate cleansers for between courses. I watch as Anna sticks to starches, eating very little. My mother keeps up a steady conversation with Anna. Now Anna is the daughter she wanted. Silvia abandoned Mother, starting a new life in America with her husband, and I am nothing but a raging disappointment.

I can't take another minute of being ignored, feeling less than, after a lifetime of following the rules and expectations laid out for me. I stand. "Excuse me, I'm very tired. I'll see you all in the morning."

"Still with the early bedtime," Lucas teases.

"She's always loved her routines and schedule," Gabriel says fondly. "Of course, only Emma wakes up bright-eyed at dawn every day." He's forgiven me for my impetuous breach of royal protocol, running from my arranged marriage. He's my big brother and he loves me.

Jackson stands with me. I paste on a smile. "Goodnight, everyone." My mother won't even look at me. Her cold dismissal infuriates me. "Goodnight, Mother."

She turns, scowling as she takes in my red halter dress, and says, "I don't even know the person in that whorish dress."

I gasp.

The room falls deathly silent.

I gather my dignity. "And I don't want to know the person who would call her own daughter a whore." I stalk out of the room, head held high. Jackson keeps pace.

"Emma," Anna calls, "please come back. Alexandra, please. This is family time." Her voice is choked. She's teary because she never had family before ours, being an orphan. She's always saying how glad she is to have us, but I'm sorry, I simply cannot stay in the same room as Mother. I am done.

Jackson is silent by my side.

"Sorry to bring you into this family disharmony," I say.

"Sorry you have family disharmony," he says. "I get the feeling it's new for you."

I gesture wildly. "As long as you do what's expected, everyone loves you. Step one toe over the line and you're a whore."

He grimaces.

The moment I get into the privacy of my suite, I head straight for the bathroom, lock the door, and burst into tears. I tried so hard to own my newfound pride in who I am. I don't want it to matter so much that my mother has shut me out because of it.

The doorknob rattles. "Babe, don't cry. Let's play guitar. Pour that into the music."

I wipe my tears, but they just keep coming. "I can't seem to stop crying. You go ahead and play." I sink to the floor and draw up my knees as another sob racks my body, heaving wrenching sobs, one after the other. A delayed reaction to grief, I don't know. I'm crying for everything I've lost and there's just so much.

A few twanging notes reach my ears between sobs and then abruptly stop. I sniffle, grab a tissue and blow my nose. One look in the bathroom mirror at my ruined smudged eye makeup, my red nose, and tearstained cheeks gets me sobbing all over again.

The door pops open a moment later. He must've picked the lock. Jackson takes me in, his eyes soft.

I try to stop crying, but I can't.

He scoops me up without a word and carries me to bed, pulling back the covers and setting me down. I curl onto my side, crying into my pillow. The light goes out and he's at my back, spooning me from behind, stroking my hair.

Finally, I run out of tears, completely exhausted. I drift off to sleep, telling myself tomorrow will be better. It was an emotional day.

Only when I wake, Jackson is gone.

His bag and guitar are gone.

There's only a scrawled note ripped from his music notepad. I read it with shaking hands.

Emma,

I'm causing more trouble than I'm worth. Make up with your family and be the person you were meant to be, a princess. Thanks for the gift of your music. Keep playing.

Jackson

This is all *her* fault. I will never forgive her.

18

———

Jackson

I'm leaving for Emma's own good. She belongs here, living the royal life, and she can't do that with me. I don't belong, her mum made it clear I don't belong, and all I'm doing is causing a bigger rift between them. It's not like Emma and I ever had a future. I was a temporary diversion from her real life.

I head for the dock with my stuff. My trip from palace to dock was uneventful. Emma slept in for once, after crying herself to sleep, so I was able to quietly leave. I found her maid, Lina, on her way up to check on Emma, concerned she'd slept in, and Lina arranged a lift to the port for me.

I board the houseboat and unlock the cabin, checking the interior for damage in my absence. It looks the same, except the rubbish was taken out for me. Images of Emma flash through my mind—finding her sleeping in my bed in that hideous wig, me trying to convince her to leave my boat while she gazed at me with her big innocent eyes. Not so innocent anymore thanks to me. I ruined her, and the least I can do is steer clear so she can rise back to the level she was born to.

I set my duffel bag and guitar case in the bedroom and

peek in the loo. Everything is soaked like it rained in here. Someone left the window open. I bet it was Emma trying to air it out after puking her guts up, and forgetting about it. Somehow I think there's always going to be reminders of her. I've never lived with a woman before, never shared a holiday with them, and I made a muck of things, didn't I?

I head to the controls and start it up. Fuel level is good. It's Christmas day, and I'm heading home. Not because I want to see my family or my mates. I need to get to the studio and record all the music I made with Emma before I lose it. It's mostly in my head—her sweet angelic voice, her melodies, countermelodies, and harmonies. I can't lose the music and her. I just can't. If I do, I won't ever get the music back again.

I have to stop overnight before finishing the trip, which is annoying, but I can't travel at night easily with the controls on this thing. I dock in northern France and see if I can make do with what remains of my nonperishable food. I've got a bag of crisps. Perfect. I shove a handful in my mouth and help myself to a glass of water. The water quickly peters out to a slow trickle and then stops. I stare at the empty faucet. What the—Emma. Had to be. She probably ran the water for an ungodly amount of time, doing who knows what, unaware that fresh water on a boat does run out. She's ignorant of real-world stuff because she's a sheltered princess. The only reason she sought out someone like me was to get a taste of how the other half lived.

Fuck it. I'll take the tequila. What's left of it after she helped herself.

I finish the crisps and the dregs of tequila, and then I sit and stare at nothing, numb, empty, not a note in my head. I'm gutted. Bloody hell.

I collapse into bed. Happy Christmas to me.

~

Emma

I'm completely numb. Jackson's abrupt departure shocked me, and then I shut down, unable to handle one more upset. I made it through Christmas, being as pleasant as possible to my family, though I couldn't manage even a polite smile. Mother and I have worked around each other. And by that I mean she has pretended I don't exist, and I have done the same. Why focus on a lost cause? I spent most of Christmas listening to a matronly aunt prattle on about me as a little girl.

Now it's the day after Christmas, and I need to go. I don't know where. I just know I cannot stay here. I feel useless in the new order of palace life. I pack a suitcase with my new wardrobe. I can't go back to Italy with the memories of Jackson there. Maybe I'll go to the US and visit Silvia and her husband. She did ask me to visit.

I consider my guitar and decide against it. It's too soon. It will only remind me of Jackson. His gravelly voice, the warmth in his eyes, his fingers on mine, guiding me to the right notes. At first I blamed Jackson's leaving on my mother's rude dismissal of him; then I blamed it on my fight with her, driving him away. That is what his note referred to, but maybe it was as simple and cold-blooded as him simply wanting my money. He had the diamond ring and there was nothing more he wanted or needed from me. Maybe it was all of the above. I have no way of knowing since he left without a goodbye. The bastard. All I have is that stupid note. I don't know where he lives. I don't have his number. I thought there'd be more time to work something out.

I gaze out the window, staring at the sea. He's probably on his boat somewhere back on his solo holiday that I interrupted. I was an inconvenience he could no longer tolerate. Dark despair seeps through every cell of my being, leaving me utterly drained. A lifetime of keeping a stiff upper lip kicks in, and I force myself to face facts. I am me with or without him. Maybe I'll discover even more cool things about myself. I'll have new experiences on my own. I'll still sing. Maybe I'll take piano lessons instead of guitar.

One foot in front of the other.

Always moving forward.

I grab my phone to text Silvia about a visit when there's a knock at my bedroom door. My heart pounds, my nerves jangling, my stomach fluttering. Maybe it's Jackson. Maybe he came back to me. "Come in!"

The door opens to Lina, and my shoulders droop in disappointment. Ridiculous. *Stop imagining he'll suddenly realize he made a mistake and run back to you.*

Lina bows her head and does a quick curtsy. "Your Highness, the queen requests you see her in her sitting room immediately."

My mind flashes to Anna and her new pregnancy. "Is she okay?"

"I believe so, ma'am."

I let out a breath of relief. "I'll be with her shortly."

"She says it's urgent, ma'am."

Heart in my throat, I head toward the door. Maybe there's a problem with the baby. She might not have confided it to the servants. I race upstairs to Anna and Gabriel's suite, praying that it's not what I fear.

I'm quickly shown inside and stop short.

My mother and Anna are seated at a round table set for tea in the sitting room. I immediately sense a trap. Worse, I sense they're a united front and I'm the odd person out.

"What is this?" I ask.

Anna smiles. "Have a seat."

I cross my arms, refusing to look at my mother. "She doesn't want me here."

"I want you here," Anna says in an unusually stern tone. "Now please have a seat before I drag you over by the hair." She smiles pleasantly.

I eye her. She's bigger than me, and I don't really want to do any defensive moves against my pregnant sister-in-law. I comply, taking the seat on Anna's other side. "Will anyone else be joining us?"

"Just us," Anna says brightly. "Now we are going to enjoy

some tea, and then we are going to fix this." She signals to her maid, who immediately sets about pouring tea for each of us. Anna thanks her and dismisses her.

"Really, Anna, this is completely unnecessary," my mother says. "There's nothing to fix."

Anna narrows her eyes. "Do not even pretend there's nothing wrong between you and Emma. I wanted to fix this yesterday, but I needed to wait because Emma was dealing with another low blow with Jackson's departure."

"I say good riddance," my mother says, looking at her nails.

My hands form fists. So callous to my pain. Has she ever cared about my feelings?

"With all due respect," Anna says to my mother, "that was incredibly rude. Emma adores that man, and you don't need to be so cold about it."

Thank you, Anna! I relax a little, knowing Anna is on my side.

"Perhaps I should leave," Mother says, rising from her chair.

I stand too. "There's nothing more that needs to be said. I'm going to visit Silvia."

"No one is going anywhere!" Anna barks. "Now sit your asses down. That is an order from your queen!"

I promptly take my seat, not wanting to upset the pregnant woman. Mother does too, though a little slower. She's used to giving commands, not taking them. She used to be queen.

Anna takes my hand and then takes Mother's hand in her other hand. "I'm sorry I had to pull rank, but you're my family now." Her eyes get teary, and that pierces my defensive state, bringing tears to my own eyes. She squeezes my hand and gives me a sympathetic look. "Listen, us Rourke women have to stick together, okay?"

I nod.

She turns to Mother, who gives a curt nod before looking away.

Anna releases our hands and straightens. "Now, Alexandra, you owe Emma an apology for your dismissal of her new empowered self, among other things. She's your daughter, she's done her duty her whole life, and she doesn't deserve to be ignored."

My mother turns to me and meets my eyes for the first time in two whole days. "I'm sorry if I've ignored you."

I clench my teeth, biting back harsh words. Her apology is half-hearted and incomplete.

"And?" Anna prompts.

Mother turns to her. "She's changed. You can't expect me to just accept this—" she waves a hand toward me "—phase. She dresses completely inappropriately for a lady of her station. It's because of that depraved rock star."

I'm wearing a bright outfit meant to cheer myself up—a red and white polka-dotted blouse with black trousers and black high-heeled boots. It is not inappropriate or depraved. It is *normal* and stylish for a woman of my age. I don't care about "my station." I'm never going back to my modest pastel dresses meant for a matronly woman again.

Before I can say any of that, Anna speaks up, smiling gently at my mother as she says, "Try again, my darling mother-in-law. I know you can do better than that. She's dressed completely fine. And Jackson is good people. Don't judge him because he looks more rock 'n roll than buttoned-up prince."

Mother sniffs. "Good people don't just up and leave without a goodbye to their hosts."

Anna gives Mother a withering look. The kind my mother is aces at. "We are not leaving this room until things are fixed between you and Emma. I have an important announcement once that business is taken care of."

We both turn to her expectantly. Is it baby news? Boy or girl? Is she having twins? Or is it some news on the day spa front or fabulous guests for the royal fantasy suite? Anna has so many interesting projects in the works.

"Got your attention now," Anna says smugly, helping herself to a blueberry scone. "Now try again."

Mother purses her lips. "Emma, I may have prematurely judged your friend."

I say nothing. It wasn't an apology, and she hasn't addressed the fact that I'm not the old prim and proper Emma anymore. That I've reclaimed myself and that self is completely appropriate. Not whorish.

Anna chomps on her scone and slurps some tea. Mother cringes and tries to hide it by taking a sip of tea.

Tense seconds tick by, the only sound Anna noisily eating and slurping. I suspect she does it to annoy Mother. I can't remember her sounding like that before at a meal.

Mother shudders at the constant chew-slurp noise and finally speaks. "Emma, I accept your apology regarding leaving Abdul. You were correct to do so, though..." She nods once. "I am just glad...well, that it is done. We will work to restore the good name of our family."

I meet her eyes, feeling it's a good start, but...

Mother goes back to her tea.

Anna's chomping and slurping mercifully stops and she coughs out, "Whorish," which is not easy to do.

Mother closes her eyes for a moment and then contemplates her tea. "It was wrong to call your dress whorish, and I will *try* to accept the unexpected changes I've seen in you." She finally lifts her gaze to mine. "You're a grown woman now, single and making your way in the world on your own, so this is to be expected."

It's more of an apology than I ever thought I'd hear from her.

Anna turns to me expectantly.

I work to sound civil. "Thank you, Mother. I hope we will one day be able to get to know each other as two adult women making our way in the world." I parrot her words back because I'm done apologizing for exploring and changing myself in a way that I've really come to enjoy. Though it occurs to me that the loss of the closeness I shared with my mother is what finally drove me to leave Abdul and seek out a new life. In some bizarre way, her distance helped me break ties with my old life. I almost want to thank her for that, but I don't think she'd take it the right way.

My mother inclines her head at me.

"Wonderful!" Anna exclaims, slapping a palm on the table. "I can feel the cloud lifting already. Oh, crap. Excuse me!" She rushes from the sitting room to her bedroom and hopefully to the bathroom because we can hear her retching through the open door.

Mother winces.

I stare at the table, wondering if I would be the same way when I'm pregnant one day, or maybe I'd be like my mother and not have any morning sickness. More fanciful fantasies. I'm single and truly free for the first time in my life. I need to focus on that no matter how much I wish things were different. No matter how much I miss Jackson.

Anna returns a few minutes later and takes her seat. "Sorry. It comes and goes very unpredictably, which brings me to my announcement. I would really like it if the two of you could get more involved with the day spa and natural beauty product line. I'm not running on all four cylinders, if you know what I mean, and there's a lot of work to be done. Gabriel wants to help, but let's face it, only we women understand what's needed in a beauty product line and spa that will mostly bring in female clientele. So, first things first, I need help with research. I need you to find the best natural products on the market. Then I need you to figure out if it's better to license existing products with our label and local ingredients, or start fresh and hire someone to come up with unique formulations. And—" she lifts a finger "—here's the part you'll probably really like. I need you to visit day spas in Europe so we know what services are expected locally and can go one level further." She slaps a hand over her mouth for a moment and then takes a deep breath. "False alarm on the puking front. You two will be my trusted team here in Europe. Silvia's going to do a little digging in the US. I can't do much travelling until I stop barfing up the heir." She smiles, rubs her stomach, and talks to it. "Just kidding, you're staying right there." She looks at me and then Mother. "Once I'm feeling better, I'll jump in again."

She grabs my hand and Mother's hand and inclines her head at me. I take Mother's other hand, so we now form a circle.

Anna leans in, her voice fierce. "Stronger together. Rourke women united for the cause, for the future of Villroy, for our legacy."

Mother lets out a shaky breath.

"Yes," I breathe, my heart soaring. I suddenly see where I fit into the new way of life here at the palace. Anna's right. Only us Rourke women know what needs to be done for a day spa, and it *is* the future of our kingdom, the key to saving our faltering economy. "I'll happily do anything you need. Count me in."

"Yay!" Anna says, releasing my hand and hugging me. She lets me go and turns to my mother. "Alexandra?"

"My God," Mother says, "you are truly one of us." She wipes her eyes. She must really be moved because she usually keeps a tight rein on her emotions. "I-I'm overcome."

"Aww, I love you," Anna says, giving her a hug.

Mother breaks down in tears, crying on Anna's shoulder. I'm frozen in shock. Even at my father's funeral, Mother didn't break down.

Mother pushes Anna away a few minutes later, saying, "Don't fuss over me." She takes a shaky breath and squares her shoulders. "Yes, I would love to assist for this worthy cause. And I know Emma will be a great help, if she doesn't mind working with me." She turns to me, her lower lip wobbling, her eyes still shiny from her recent cry.

Now I'm crying. "Of course I will. I've missed you so much."

"Well, geez," Anna says, her own eyes watering. "If I'd known all it took to bring Alexandra back to the living was getting knocked up, I would've made Gabriel get on it earlier."

"Anna," Mother chides gently, but she's smiling.

"Ha! Just kidding," Anna says with a wink. "He tried every chance he could get. The man is hot for me."

Mother presses her lips together primly. "May we talk about the beauty product line now?"

Anna pulls a huge white binder out from under the table. "All right, ladies, let's get down to business."

I exchange a smile with my mother, a peace settling over me. I know my place, and I know I'm important to the cause. I'll learn to love this new life and, eventually, I'll learn how to live without Jackson.

19

——————

Emma

It's New Year's Eve and I can't shake my sadness. I know I have so much to look forward to in the new year ahead of me. I have an important job helping Anna with the day spa; in many ways it's a fun job. I have music and a new closeness with Anna and my mother. Hopefully, Silvia too, who will be joining us for some of our spa visits in Europe, using some of her vacation days.

It's quiet here in the private salon, the TV on low volume showing New Year's Eve celebrations around the world. My brothers are out partying who knows where, so it's just me, Gabriel, Anna, and Mother. I'm sitting on a long burgundy leather sofa next to Anna and Gabriel. Mother sits in a high-back chair adjacent to us. In deference to Anna's pregnancy, we're all sipping sparkling water.

"No one ever plays the piano in the conservatory," I say, thinking of my new passion for music. "Maybe we should move it in here." The conservatory is a distant, largely empty formal room that was once host to an evening's entertainment in the olden days before all the other forms of entertainment available now.

"No one plays," Gabriel says.

"I used to play," my mother says.

This is news to me. "You did? Why did you stop?"

She lifts one shoulder. "I guess I was too busy with my duties as queen and with all of you. Seven children running around the palace took a lot of my focus and energy. It seemed taking time for myself was selfish when I was needed for more important things." Only now she's not queen and all of us kids are full grown.

"You should play again," I say. "Did you have lessons?"

"When I was a child," she says, waving that away. "I'm so rusty I'm sure it would be like starting all over again."

"We should both learn," I say. "We'll move the piano to this cozier spot and find a teacher."

"And then you could put on a concert for us!" Anna exclaims.

"Oh, no," Mother and I say at the same time. I suppose we're both shy about our skills. We exchange a smile.

The door opens to our butler, Nolan. "Excuse me, Your Majesties, for the interruption. Mr. Jackson Walker is here, asking to see Emma." He turns to me. "Should I let him in, Your Highness?"

Heart in my throat, I can't manage a word, so I just nod. The minute he leaves, I turn to Anna. "How do I look?"

She kisses her fingertips. "Perfection."

I smooth my hair back behind my ears. "Really?" I'm wearing no makeup, dressed casually in a thick cream wool sweater with black leggings. The outfit was a Christmas gift from Anna, who's been encouraging me to dress casually at home for maximum comfort. It has been a decadent experience.

Anna grins. "I'd do you."

Gabriel barks out a laugh. My mother frowns. Anna's outrageousness can never be tamed. I think that's what my brother loves about her. I'm still getting used to it.

I stand and smooth my sweater down and then sit again. I set my hands on my lap and then fold them together, but that seems too posed and proper. I lift my hands. "I don't know what to do with my hands."

"Awww," Anna says, slinging an arm around my shoulders and giving me a squeeze. "You're so cute." She lets me go and gazes directly into my eyes. "Relax. Play it cool. Listen to what he has to say and go from there."

"Should we go?" Gabriel asks.

My mother huffs. "Why should we disrupt our evening for an uninvited visitor?"

Oh, God. I can see it now. My mother as witness to an emotional painful talk with Jackson. The bastard left without a goodbye. Only that stupid note. I should burn that note. Maybe I should go to the front hall. This could be extremely awkward in front of my family. Also, why is he here? What does it mean?

I stand and head for the door to the salon just as it opens to the man who stole my heart. His familiar features haunt my dreams, and now he's here in vivid reality. I take in his dirty-blond hair, cropped close on the sides, his tired-looking blue eyes, his strained expression, his scruffy beard, his leather jacket. He's carrying his guitar case.

"Emma." His gravelly voice scrapes against all my raw nerves.

I lift my chin. "What are you doing here?"

"I wrote you a song."

"You *left* me." I hate that my voice shakes.

He frowns. "That was a mistake. I regret…can I just play for you? It's all in the song, everything I want to say."

"Let's hear it!" Anna shouts from across the room. The TV is silenced.

Jackson meets my eyes in question.

I tell myself to stay strong. "If you like."

He pulls out his guitar, attaches a strap, and slips it over his shoulder, strumming a few notes. He's standing in front of me, heart in his eyes, and I can already feel myself melting. I'm too easy. He hurt me deeply.

And then he begins to sing in his deep gravelly voice, a ballad he wrote just for me.

"I ran from you and I was a fool
How can I run from my very soul?
My heart stays with you
I need to be whole
I need my Emma
My goddess of music
My Emma
My muse, my life
I would be your family man
My Emma
Will you be my wife?"

The last note rings out pure and sincere, and I'm frozen in shock.

His gaze searches mine.

I can't quite believe my ears. My heart hammers against my rib cage, my pulse thrumming through my veins. "What?" I ask inanely as if hearing him propose again would suddenly make sense to me.

He removes his guitar, setting it in its case, and then drops to his knees in front of me. "Emma, will you marry me?"

My mouth goes dry. He proposed again. I'm having trouble wrapping my mind around it. "You left me and now you want to marry me?"

He takes my hands in his. "I thought you'd be better off without me in the picture. But, Emma, I love you, and I can't turn my back on us. This past week has been excruciating. Bloody horrific. I didn't think I could ever join my life with someone, but you're different, so special. I know I'll never find another woman like you. I want everything with you, marriage, kids, music that we write and play and sing together for the rest of our lives."

I stare at him, speechless.

He rises smoothly to his feet and gazes deep into my eyes.

"I love you." His voice breaks. "It's been hell. Everything reminds me of you, my guitar, my boat, even my stupid leather jacket because you wore it once. I can't sleep at night. I'm miserable without you."

Part of me is pleased that he's in misery, though it was his own fault. The other part of me is filled with hope. "You shouldn't have left, especially without a goodbye."

"I thought I was making things worse for you with your mum. I thought you belonged here and I didn't, but we belong together no matter where that is. I swear on my life I will never leave you again. I love you more than I love music, more than I love myself. I never thought I'd feel that way about anyone."

A lightness spreads through my limbs, a soft floating feeling that I've only ever felt with music and Jackson. The two are forever entwined for me now. "Swear on your guitar that you won't flake."

He takes the guitar from its case and hands it to me. "It's yours. Everything I have is yours."

I set the guitar gently back in its case, avoiding eye contact as I ask the one thing that has nagged at me. "What about the diamond ring? Would you give it back to me?"

"Um…"

I straighten and force myself to voice my fear. "If I wasn't a royal with money, would you still want me?"

He steps close. "Yes. But I can't give you back that ring. I need it to set up a trust for Charlie's son. He's only four. Emma, he named him for me. Jack." His voice chokes, his eyes watering. "I want to make sure he has a chance at a good life, music lessons, tutors, whatever he needs."

My knees go weak. He wasn't using me at all. He was looking out for a child who lost his father much too young. How could I not love this man?

He takes both my hands in his. "Does any part of my song sound remotely good to you?"

"Yes."

One corner of his mouth lifts in a crooked endearing

smile. "Which part?"

I grab him and hug him, my entire body relaxing back in Jackson's arms, wrapped in his heat, his scent, his love. "All of it. Yes to all of it."

He cups my jaw and kisses me gently before hugging me tight again. "I love you, Emma."

"I love you too."

"I want you to pick out your engagement ring this time," he whispers in my ear. "Everything exactly *your* style."

I can't help my beaming smile. Jackson has been nothing but supportive of my efforts to explore new interests and discover my own personal style.

"Congratulations!" Anna cheers, rushing over to us. She hugs me and then him, beaming at us. "I'm so happy for you guys!"

"Thank you!" I say, pleased that at least she is. I glance over at my mother and Gabriel. My brother smiles. "Congratulations, Emma." He gives Jackson a curt nod. "Jackson." That's just Gabriel's way. He's not over-the-top with enthusiasm like Anna.

Anna returns to her place at Gabriel's side. Mother remains quiet.

I take Jackson's hand, confiding quietly, "I've made up with my mother. It wasn't you that was the cause of our disagreement. It went much deeper than that. Next time you should communicate your concerns with me."

He lifts my hand, brushing a kiss over the back of my knuckles, his blue eyes intent on mine. "I'm a virgin to relationships. Be gentle with me, love. I'll try hard to catch up."

My cheeks flush, thinking of how he helped me catch up in the sexiest of ways. "I'm pretty new to them too. We'll figure it out as long as we stick together. Come on, I want you to say hello to Mother. She needs to get used to you. Make sure you bow your head and use proper address."

He entwines his fingers with mine, murmuring, "Got it." I lead him over to greet my mother.

"Hello, Your Highness," Jackson says, dipping his head.

"I hope that we can get to know each other a little better. I'll be good to Emma."

I can't help my smile.

Mother is not smiling. "Where will you live?"

"I have a place in London," Jackson says.

I turn to him. "Actually, I have a lot of work to do here. I'm helping Anna with the new day spa and beauty product line."

"It's important work," my mother puts in, eyeing Jackson for his response.

"I'll rent a cottage nearby," Jackson says. "Whatever Emma wants."

"Then I won't stand in your way," Mother says. "Congratulations to you both." She stands. "Good night, everyone."

Anna grabs Gabriel's hand. "We're going to give you two some privacy."

The three of them file out, having a hushed conversation. Probably just as shocked at the turn of events as I am.

Jackson gives my hand a tug, leading me to the sofa. He gives me a small smile. "I can't believe you forgave me so quickly. I was prepared for a long hard campaign to win you back."

"I'm surprised I lasted as long as I did. I wanted to take you back the first moment I clapped eyes on you. I've missed you terribly."

He slides an arm around my shoulders and pulls me close. "My emotions have been so raw and I couldn't channel them into the music until I made it about you. You were the missing piece that made me whole again."

"Oh, Jackson." My eyes sting with tears. He's a poet under that rough edgy exterior. "You're killing me with all this heartfelt emotional stuff. I'm not used to it and I'm certainly not good at returning the same."

He tips my chin up and kisses me. "You don't have to be the same as me. Just be with me. That's all I need."

"Okay," I whisper. And then he's kissing me and there are no more words, only love and desire and a bone-deep sense of rightness. His hand slides down my throat, down my sides, and then he's lifting me and settling me on his lap, straddling him. The kiss turns carnal, his hands sliding up my sweater, cupping my breasts, pinching my nipples. A moan escapes.

He breaks the kiss, breathing hard. "Let's go somewhere more private, yeah?"

I climb off his lap and take his hand, walking with him toward the hallway. "I'd like you to live at the palace with me. It's the best place for me to get my work done, and we can set up a music studio for you in the conservatory."

He halts. "I feel strange here, like I'm trespassing. My people would've been the servants."

I meet his gaze and say evenly, "And I'm sure I'll feel strange in the front row at your concerts while women scream over you, but that is the deal in a committed relationship. You deal with my strange, and I deal with yours."

He presses his lips together, his blue eyes dancing with amusement. "Yours is stranger."

I lift my chin. "That remains to be seen."

He frames my face with both hands. "You know how you would've taken me back the moment you saw me?"

"Yes."

"I would've done anything to keep you in my life. So it turns out I'm just as easy as you."

I can't help my smile. "Wait. Do you mean I'm easy as in loose like a hussy?" I put some outrage into my voice because I *love* the idea.

His words run hot across my lips. "That's exactly what I mean, love. I'm a lucky man."

"Remember that."

He kisses me tenderly. "How can I forget when your eyes are hazy with lust every time you clap eyes on me?"

I throw my arms around his neck and kiss him passionately. And then I take his hand and lead him deep into the palace to the privacy of my room, where I plan to keep him for the foreseeable future.

EPILOGUE

Three months later...

Emma

I am beyond excited on this glorious spring day so full of promise and potential. It's the first Monday in April and we're about to break ground on the day spa. Jackson's band, Ignite, is here to play after the ribbon cutting. And a ton of people have showed up to hear them play; many of them could be future clients for the spa. I don't worry about his many female fans because my faith in Jackson is absolute. It's really not difficult. He shows me his love every time he looks at me, every time his gravelly voice sings for me, every time he touches me. As Anna likes to say, the man is hot for me.

We live at the palace in my suite, and Jackson has gradually become more comfortable. My brothers come and go, but when they're home, they love to spend time with Jackson. Gabriel and Anna have accepted him as family, even though our wedding is still a couple of months off, and my mother has warmed to him, as he's proven his commitment to me by living where I've asked him to live, by composing song after song about me and our love, and by treating her respectfully. Plus it's obvious how happy he makes me. I've got a song in my heart and a bounce in my step. Jackson has commissioned a home for us in nearby France. It's private and sheltered, much like the Italian villa where we fell in love, and outfitted with a music studio.

Now that the research stage is complete and Anna is feeling better from her morning sickness, the Rourke team will be ramping up local manufacturing for the new beauty product line and getting our fishing industry involved. Many of the cosmetics will feature local ingredients, including fish oil, algae, sponges, and sea salt. In the meantime, Anna is still booking ladies' weeks and honeymoon guests for the royal fantasy suite. She charges exorbitantly for the privilege.

"Emma! Come on, it's time!" Anna shouts cheerfully, gesturing for me to join her at the fat red ribbon in front of the future day spa location. It's on the east side of the island, closest to France. Anna has plans to build a dock here, redirecting the ferry for visitors. The port on the southern end of the island will be used solely for the fishing and cosmetics industry.

I suppress a cringe at Anna's outburst. Mother does it for me. It's just that Anna is queen now and should contain her volume. The press is here, along with the public. Gabriel merely smiles, enjoying her natural enthusiasm. He's so far gone in love it's ridiculous. I know this stupid-in-love feeling well.

I join Anna at the ribbon, my mother by my side. Mother is dressed in a youthful light blue silk dress with a red and blue floral pattern. With all the day spa visits Mother and I made together, along with digging deep into beauty treatments, Mother looks younger and more vibrant than I can ever remember. She's received her fair share of compliments at the spas too, many of the aestheticians commenting on her flawless complexion and youthful appearance, some even saying we could be sisters. I wouldn't go that far. She didn't buy the flattery for a minute, but I think it did boost her confidence, along with having a purpose through our work. She's fifty-four with a new vitality and energy. Maybe she too needed to find her place in the new palace order. Of course, she still misses my father, we all do, and she mentions him often, but it's more with fondness than with the sharp pain of fresh grief.

Anna beams and hugs us both at the same time. "Ah! This is so exciting!" She's glowing with good health, five months pregnant. "We'll all put a hand on the scissors handle for the picture. I want everyone to know the Rourke women were the ones who got this project off the ground."

"Gabriel should be in the picture," my mother says pointedly. "He is the king, and this is an event for the kingdom."

"Of course!" Anna gestures him over. "Behind every successful woman, there's a good man."

I stifle a laugh. I'm sure Gabriel would say the reverse.

A servant brings over a giant pair of scissors with black handles. They're comically large, but I guess it will look good in the picture. We all line up, Gabriel behind Anna, then Mother in front of her, and me in the very front. We're in height order.

The reporters jostle for space, all cameras aimed at us.

Someone hands Anna a microphone. "Can I have your attention, please," she says and waits for silence. "On this momentous spring day, a time of new beginnings, I am proud to break ground on Villroy's long-awaited day spa."

The crowd breaks into applause.

Anna goes on. "This would not have been possible without the dedicated hard work of Princess Alexandra, Princess Emma, and Princess Silvia. Let's all give them a hand." Silvia isn't here, but it's nice that Anna acknowledges her contribution.

More applause and Jackson's whistle rising above it. I beam at him, where he's standing on stage with his band. He points to me, mouthing, "You rock!"

I smile. He claims I'm rock 'n roll with my ballads, though I think he brings them to that level. He's an extraordinary musician. Just in the time I've known him I've witnessed him reach new levels of musicianship. The fire is back in his belly, that deep passion for the music.

Anna hands Gabriel the microphone. His deep voice full of rough authority rings out. "I hereby dedicate the Island Bliss Spa on behalf of the kingdom of Villroy. And we want you all back here for the grand opening in June!"

"Now!" Anna yells.

We lower the scissor handle, cutting the ribbon in half. Camera flashes light up in front of my eyes as everyone cheers. Ignite launches into their raucous number one hit, "Inferno," shooting the energy of the crowd to a high pitch.

Anna and Gabriel are hugging, and then she rushes over to hug me and Mother too. "We did it, ladies!" she exclaims. "And in other fab news, the doctor says the heir is an heiress. We're having a girl!"

"Congratulations!" I exclaim. "More women for the Rourke team!"

Anna laughs. "Right on. I've got you drinking the Kool-Aid." She turns to Mother, who's been quiet. "Alexandra?"

"I'm so happy for you," Mother says, her voice cracking. Her lower lip wobbles and Anna pulls her in for a hug, offering privacy for the leaking tears. She's taller than my mother, so Mother's face is hidden a bit. Mother has taken all of the pregnancy news quite personally. She's very excited to be a grandmother.

I bounce on the balls of my feet, exuberant with all the wonderful news and what I'm about to do. "I've got to go see my love. Congratulations again!"

Mother pulls away from Anna and wipes her eyes. "Can't you listen from here? It's quite loud enough."

"I need to get a little closer."

"She's in love," Anna says. "She always needs to get a little closer. Get it, girl."

I laugh and dash off, heading behind the raised stage set up for Ignite's performance. My guitar is waiting for me there on a stand. I slip the strap over my shoulder and admire the smooth rosewood of my guitar, humming a little under my breath.

Their song ends and Jackson says into the microphone,

"Now I'd like to introduce to you the love of my life, my inspiration, my heart and soul, Emma Rourke!"

I walk on stage on shaky legs, belatedly nervous. I've been working with a vocal teacher to broaden my range and tonal quality, yet this is my first public performance. It's also the first time my family has heard me sing since I was little. All of my lessons have been in the conservatory, far from the hustle of palace life.

Jackson smiles at me, love shining in his blue eyes, and I focus solely on him, my heart slowing from hummingbird range to a steady thump. He turns to the crowd. "This is an Emma original. I'll let her tell you about it."

I lean close to the microphone in front of me on its stand. "Hello, everyone." Feedback rings out from standing too close to it. "Sorry. This song is called 'The Veil' and it's about what happens when the veil over our eyes drops and reveals something new."

"Jackson!" a woman screams at a hair-raising volume.

Jackson doesn't react, merely turns to me. "Let's hear it, love." He starts playing. It's a duet, and I know he'll join me in the chorus.

I begin to play, singing just for him, my audience of one. His eyes close, his expression pure joy at the music we make together. It fills me up, our shared love. Soon the music lifts me and suddenly I'm soaring. I turn to the audience and sing strong and sure, pouring myself into the music that means so much to me. I am the woman who ripped off all the veils— the bridal veil, my palace veil, my proper princess veil—and returned to myself in a wholly new empowered way as a bride-to-be, a contributing palace member, a princess, and a musician.

I am music. I am love. I am Emma.

I ROAR!

The song ends and I come back to reality with a start as applause rings in my ears.

Jackson's voice rumbles near my ear. "Beautiful. Take a bow."

I bow my head and do a small curtsy, my upbringing kicking in with the tremendous shock of applause that only seems to grow. Someone wolf-whistles and I turn to see Gabriel, Anna, and my mother at the side of the stage in an area cordoned off with red velvet rope, smiling and clapping. Guards stand behind them.

I lift a hand to them in appreciation and make my exit, leaving Ignite to do their thing.

"Isn't she amazing?" Jackson asks the crowd. "That's my angel. I fell in love with her voice, and the rest of it, all that makes her so amazing, is the gift of my life. Emma Rourke, everyone."

The applause keeps going. The energy of the crowd flows through me in an exhilarating rush. My cheeks flush, my pulse thrumming through my veins. This is how Jackson must feel performing for an enthusiastic crowd.

I put my guitar back in its case nearby and rejoin my family at the side of the stage.

"You were awesome!" Anna exclaims.

"Wonderful," Gabriel says.

"I had no idea you could sing like that, Emma," Mother says. "If I'd known, I would've encouraged you more musically instead of pursuing languages."

I smile. "I love them both, music and languages. And you gave me everything I needed. It was up to me to find what brings me happiness."

Mother tilts her head. "I understand better what you and Jackson have in common." The music onstage rises in volume with Jackson's killer electric guitar riff. Mother winces. "Though his usual music is quite jarring."

"It's growing on me," I say with a smile. "Could you hold onto this?" I ask Gabriel, holding out my guitar case.

The moment he takes it, I join the audience, elbowing my way to the front row and screaming like the ultimate fangirl. I lift my arms in the air and dance.

~

Jackson

I'm in a tux standing barefoot on the beach on Villroy Island on a perfect June day, about to marry my angel. If you had asked me a year ago if I thought this would be my life, that would've been a hell no. I was grieving Charlie, grieving the loss of my music, lost in dark despair. But now my future is bright. I'm about to marry my soul mate, do the whole family-man thing, and commit body, heart, and soul. This thing with Emma is better than money, better than fame, better than applause. It's real and raw, a life filled with music and love. Creating music has never been easier. I delivered the new record to the label on time. It wasn't well received at first. They thought it was too different from Ignite's previous albums to put out. It did feature Emma's voice prominently and have more blues and ballads than my usual. All's well. My manager renegotiated the contract, and they put it out as a solo album under my name with the others credited as special guest musicians. Now our contract is finished. They're letting Ignite go, and we're all cool with that. I can't be the guy I used to be with Ignite, none of us can without Charlie. We're no longer a band so much as mates who play together whenever we can. Maybe little Jack, Charlie's son, will join us one day. He's starting piano lessons now that he's all set with his trust.

I take in a deep breath of salty sea air. The press's fascination has died down with me and Emma since we mostly lie low doing our own thing. There was no official royal announcement for our wedding in order to ensure our privacy. Apparently, Emma marrying on the beach instead of in the palace chapel is a huge break with tradition. She's the first princess to choose to marry outside the chapel in the Rourke family history. That's my Emma, forging her own path. We have security, of course, being out in the open like this, and a small guest list. My mum and brother are here, along with my brother's wife and kids. My family is much more impressed with Emma as a royal than they've ever been with me as a rock star. Mum even admitted to being starstruck just meeting her. Emma immediately pointed out my finer qualities. "Jackson is an exceptional musician and a wonderful person. He's the star, not me."

What can I say, the woman adores me.

My former bandmates, John and Max, are playing in the background for the processional as Emma's sister, Silvia, goes down the aisle, her matron of honor. I've chosen Lucas for my best man. We've become close as he's spent more time at the palace, getting more involved in the business side of things for the new industry on Villroy. I couldn't choose one best man among my bandmates, and my brother and I have never been close.

The song changes to "Emma," the first song I wrote for her. She chose it to be her song to walk down the aisle. She appears on her brother Gabriel's arm. No veil for my Emma. As her song says, she's finished with any kind of veil, real or metaphorical. She's wearing a diamond tiara that makes her look especially royal and a dark pink sleeveless gown with a keyhole cutout that shows off her cleavage. It's sexy and surprising just like her. She meets my eyes, a smile playing across her lips. Raw emotion clogs my throat, my eyes watering. *Hell. Don't cry. Don't you be the crying groom.* I scrunch my watering eyes closed and open them just as Emma starts toward me, smiling at me with a knowing look.

The woman gets me. She knows I'm trying to keep it together and she knows why—I love her like crazy.

Her smile gets wider the closer she gets, lighting up her face. She's happy to marry me, and I'm so damn lucky.

The moment Gabriel steps away, leaving Emma all to me, I cup her cheek and kiss her. I don't care that I'm supposed to wait until she's declared my wife.

"You're beautiful," I whisper.

She smiles. "Thank you. You look very handsome in your tux."

The ceremony is a blur, all of me tuned in to Emma as the minister buzzes in the background, prompting us for rings and vows. The flush to her cheeks, the pale pink of her luscious lips, the gold ring in her hazel eyes, her angelic sweet voice.

"I now pronounce you husband and wife," the minister announces.

Our guests cheer.

Emma wraps her arms around my neck, and I kiss her passionately, dipping her over my arm. My love, my life, my Emma.

I let her back up again, and she laughs. "That was some kiss!" she exclaims.

I pull her close and whisper in her ear, "Just wait for tonight."

"Maybe we can sneak away sooner," she says, grabbing my hand and striding down the aisle.

More cheers follow, confetti floating over us as the band launches into our Ignite hit "Inferno."

Emma sings along to the song that was once too much for her sensibilities. She used to say it was raucous and jangled her nerves. Ha. She's let loose and never been happier. She tells me that every time I tease her about her prim and proper ways. They pop up now and then, the manners and decorum drilled into her from birth. Which is why we're spending our wedding night away from the palace on the royal yacht. She wanted the reminder of our first nautical experience (though at a much more luxurious level), and then we'll be cruising along the South of France and to Italy. It's gorgeous this time of year.

"Check out our cake," she says, pulling me over to a long table filled with all kinds of pastries. In the center is a three-tiered white cake with a figure of a couple on top that looks remarkably like me and Emma. The rocker and the princess —me with my electric guitar wearing a black shirt pushed up to the elbows and ripped jeans, and Emma wearing a tiara and a pink gown. Even our decoration looks crazy in love. Wait a minute, is that...I peer closer. "Cocoa Puffs!"

"I had them added just for you." She grins and admires

the Cocoa Puffs ringing the edges of each tier. "I thought you should have your favorite food at our wedding."

"Brilliant!"

"I can't wait to smash it in your face."

I stare at her. "Now how is that going to look in our wedding album?"

She grimaces. "Bloody hell! Now look what's happened. You've turned into a traditionalist."

I laugh. "Maybe I'd rather spread the icing over you. Naked."

Her eyes light up, her voice husky. "Dirty, filthy man." She kisses me, her tongue sliding inside, completely uninhibited despite our nearby guests.

I break the kiss. "Later." Someone claps me on the shoulder and I turn. "Hey."

"Congratulations," Lucas says.

"Thanks, mate," I say.

"Thank you," Emma says. "We're very happy."

Lucas leans close to Emma, saying in a low teasing tone, "Running from one altar to another so quick, Emma. What will people think?"

Emma scratches her cheek with her middle finger.

I can't help but laugh. I taught her that. "It's been seven months between altars," I tell Lucas. "When it's right, it's right. I wish the same happiness for you."

He looks horrified. "Bite your tongue. You trying to jinx me? Haven't you heard I'm the world's most eligible royal bachelor? The internet voted and I won." He smiles smugly. "They say I'm charming."

Emma rolls her eyes. "You probably voted for yourself a thousand times."

He crosses his arms and smirks. "Didn't need to. I had it in the bag."

I sock him on the shoulder. "Man, I can't wait to see the woman who brings you to your knees."

He straightens, speaking in a haughty voice. "I'm a

prince, Jackson. We don't drop to our knees for anyone except the king and queen."

I grin. "Then I can't wait to meet your future queen."

I exchange a look with Emma, both of us smiling. We know how crazy love can make you.

A ghost of worry crosses Lucas's face before he says, "Not likely." He gives us a jaunty salute and heads off to the bar with his brothers.

We make the rounds, greeting our guests and accepting many warm congratulations. After a seafood dinner under the setting sun, the lights are turned on inside a tent where a dance floor has been set up.

My band is playing a special set for the reception, all of my and Emma's songs. No one is on the dance floor, and I decide we should take advantage.

"Time for our dance," I tell her, leading her onto the dance floor. It's a slow song, one of our newer songs. As soon as our house is completed with its sound studio, I'm going to record an album with her. Just us. A duo. We'll put it out on our own for total creative control.

She smiles. "You know, this is the first time I've danced with you. All that music and we never danced."

I wrap my arms around her waist and pull her close. Her arms wrap around my neck, her soft curves pressed against me. "We tried once, remember? The first night we got back together on New Year's Eve."

She grins. "Oh, I remember now. You were trying to be all sweet loving and I was trying to be all dirty grinding." She does a subtle grind against me, and I go rock hard.

"That's right," I manage.

"Now we'll just have to torture each other all night dancing as foreplay."

I stifle a groan as her hand roams over my chest. She gets me going so easily, my body remembering all the passion from each joining, and ramping up for more.

She strokes the hair at the nape of my neck. "Unless," she

whispers in a husky voice, "we sneak away for a quick hard fuck in a secret hiding place I know."

I wink. "I know it too."

She laughs, low and sexy. "Rock and roll, babe."

That's her way of saying anything goes. She's so fucking perfect.

A short while later, it's cake time and Emma is giving me *the look*. The one that says I want you. Now.

I hold her off, though she's so bloody tempting the way she presses herself against my side. I lean down and whisper in her ear, "We have to do the cake thing. It's going in our wedding album. Think of our kids. They're going to want to see it."

She beams. "Right after cake, we sneak away."

I can't deny her, can't deny myself.

We slowly slice a gigantic piece of cake, feed each other—no smashing-in-the-face rubbish—and smile for the camera.

"Ready?" I ask.

She nods. "Just one more thing I need to show our kids." She grabs our figure right off the top of the cake. "It's so us. I will treasure it forever."

My eyes sting. I frame her beautiful face with both hands and kiss her tenderly. She nips my lower lip, kissing me roughly, the intensity ratcheting up instantly.

I toss her over my shoulder and head back toward the palace. People are whistling and cheering, but I tune in to Emma's hissed, "Yessss!"

That's my Emma.

Don't miss the next book in the series *Royal Charmer*, where Lucas meets his future queen!

Alice

First thing you should know about me—I'm on my honeymoon on Villroy Island without my groom, which was a no brainer given how my ex-fiancé decided to "accidentally" fall in love with my best friend. I don't want to talk about it.

Second thing: I'm a romance author on a generously extended deadline, and I've sworn to use this time away productively. So far my editor has hated all of my ideas featuring the crushing of men. Romance is dead within my blackened heart.

I'm about to admit defeat when a prince with an image problem falls into my lap. And for some crazy reason, it's decided that me posing as his fiancée would be a good idea. The last thing I want is to actually be committed to someone, but a fake engagement may make this next book write itself.

Lucas

I enjoy being the world's most eligible royal bachelor (the internet voted and I won), but that's not all I am. I want to contribute to the kingdom, be part of the legacy. I should be the CEO of our new business venture, but my oldest brother, Gabriel, the king, blocks me at every turn, convinced I'm too flighty.

So when Gabriel's wife, Anna, the unconventional queen offers me a chance to prove myself with the bankers, and the only catch is bringing along a fake fiancée, I don't have to think twice.

Playing at fiancé is easy, until suddenly it isn't, and all I can think about is getting closer to her. Why did I have to fall for a woman afraid to get involved?

Sign up for my newsletter to be emailed when *Royal Charmer* releases at kyliegilmore.com/newsletter

ALSO BY KYLIE GILMORE

Happy Endings Book Club Series

Hidden Hollywood (Book 1)

Inviting Trouble (Book 2)

So Revealing (Book 3)

Formal Arrangement (Book 4)

Bad Boy Done Wrong (Book 5)

Mess With Me (Book 6)

Resisting Fate (Book 7)

Chance of Romance (Book 8)

Wicked Flirt (Book 9)

An Inconvenient Plan (Book 10)

A Happy Endings Wedding (Book 11)

The Clover Park Series

The Opposite of Wild (Book 1)

Daisy Does It All (Book 2)

Bad Taste in Men (Book 3)

Kissing Santa (Book 4)

Restless Harmony (Book 5)

Not My Romeo (Book 6)

Rev Me Up (Book 7)

An Ambitious Engagement (Book 8)

Clutch Player (Book 9)

A Tempting Friendship (Book 10)

Clover Park Bride: A Clover Park Short

A Valentine's Day Gift (Book 11)

Maggie Meets Her Match (Book 12)

The Clover Park STUDS Series

Almost Over It (Book 1)

Almost Married (Book 2)

Almost Fate (Book 3)

Almost in Love (Book 4)

Almost Romance (Book 5)

Almost Hitched (Book 6)

The Rourkes Series

Royal Catch (Book 1)

Royal Hottie (Book 2)

Royal Darling (Book 3)

Royal Charmer (Book 4)

Royal Player (Book 5)

Royal Shark (Book 6)

ABOUT THE AUTHOR

Kylie Gilmore is the *USA Today* bestselling author of the Rourkes series, the Happy Endings Book Club series, the Clover Park series, and the Clover Park STUDS series. She writes humorous romance that makes you laugh, cry, and reach for a cold glass of water.

Kylie lives in New York with her family, two cats, and a nutso dog. When she's not writing, wrangling kids, or dutifully taking notes at writing conferences, you can find her flexing her muscles all the way to the high cabinet for her secret chocolate stash.

Thanks for reading *Royal Darling*. I hope you enjoyed it. Would you like to know about new releases? You can sign up for my new release email list at kyliegilmore.com/newsletter. I promise not to clog your inbox! Only new release info, sales, and some fun giveaways.

I love to hear from readers! You can find me at:
    kyliegilmore.com
    Instagram.com/kyliegilmore
    Facebook.com/KylieGilmoreToo
    Twitter @KylieGilmoreToo

If you liked Jackson and Emma's story, please leave a review on your favorite retailer's website or Goodreads. Thank you.

www.ingramcontent.com/pod-product-compliance
Lightning Source LLC
Chambersburg PA
CBHW070942180726

48291CB00004B/1097